American Beauties

FAMOUS CARS IN SOUND AND VISION

e·a·r BOOKS

ISBN: 3-937406-06-9

Art Direction and Design by Sven Grot & Inken Kramp / B-99
Photo-Editorial: Franziska Gebhardt
Text-Editorial: Stefan Böckler / B-99
Special-Car-Infos: Helge Thomsen

Produced by optimal MEDIA PRODUCTION GmbH, Röbel, Germany

Printed and manufactured in Germany

EarBooks is a project of edel CLASSICS GmbH

www.earbooks.net

FOREWORD

Do you know a more glamorous embodiment of the American Way of Life than a classic American limousine? Whole generations of teenagers lost their virginity on the back seats of such automobiles. They were the epitome of freedom and untamed masculinity. Stars and wannabees have all bathed in their aura of wealth, beauty and success. The passion for automobiles shaped the profile of an entire continent and cast a spell over people worldwide too. Join us on a fascinating journey with the legendary icons of the road: American Beauties.

A CAR, A JOB,
A GIRL, A HOUSE.

1957 Chevrolet Bel Air (coverphoto)
Five American Beauties – one of them a 1947 Pontiac Streamliner

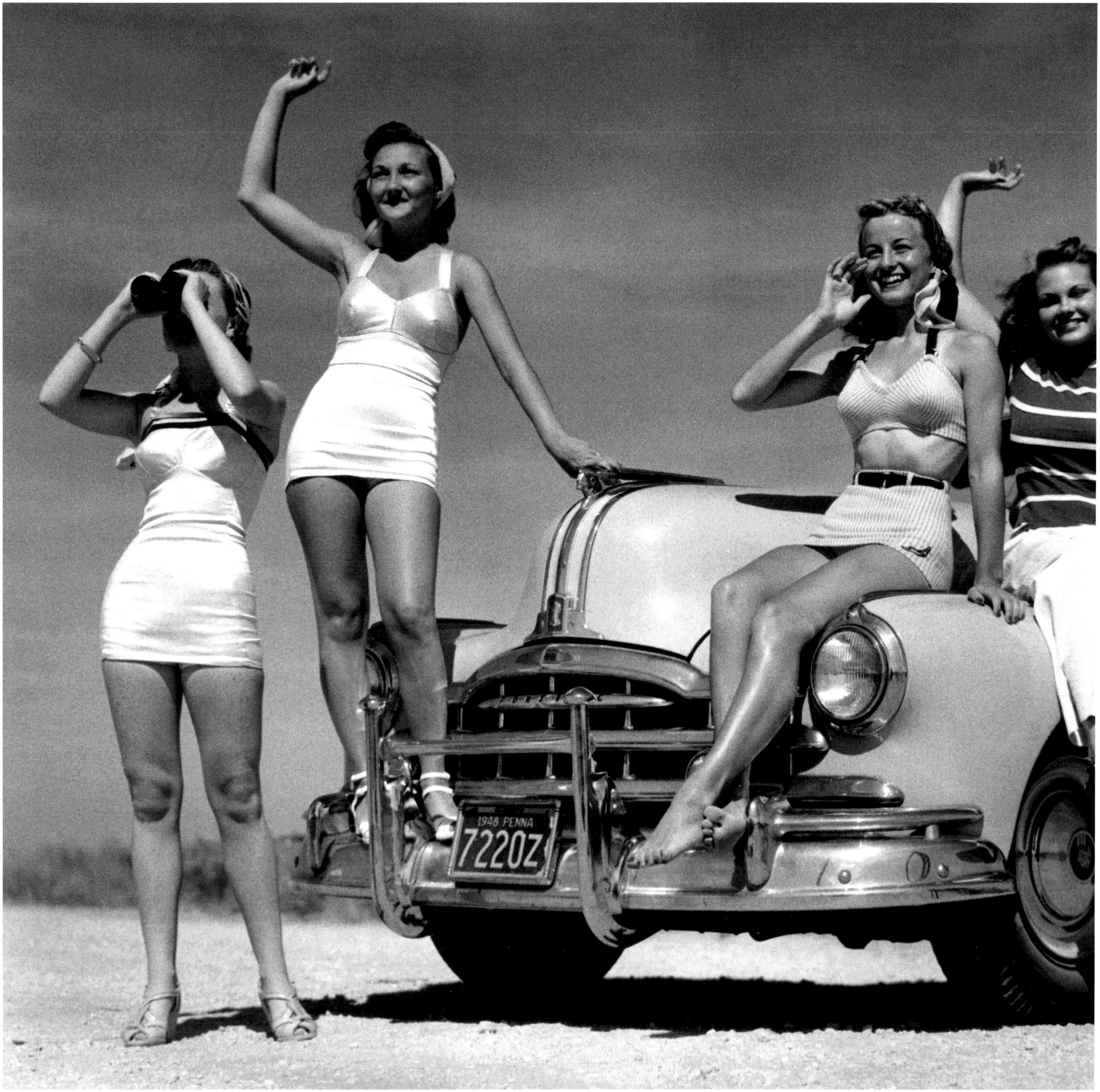
1948 PENNA
7220Z

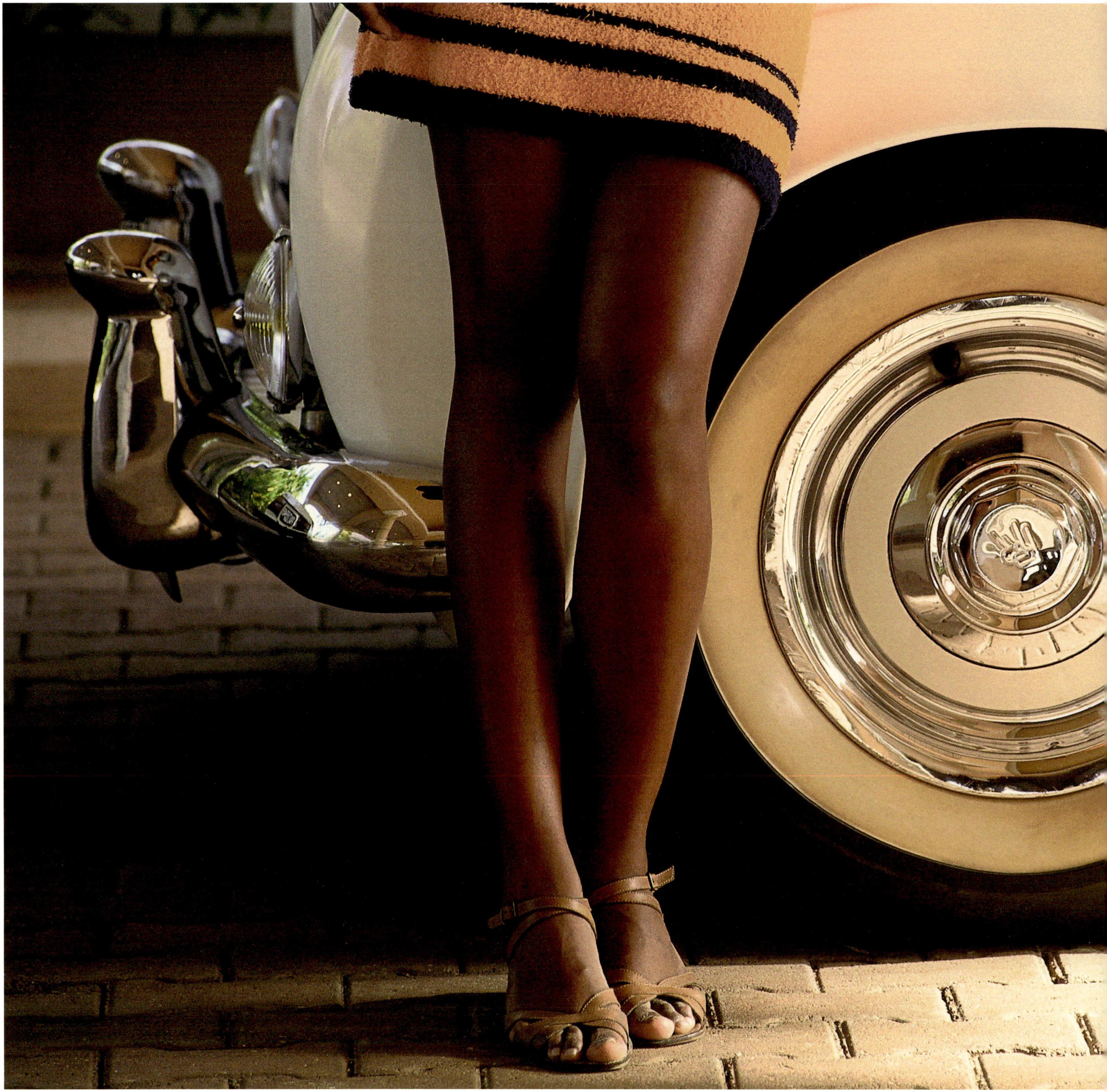

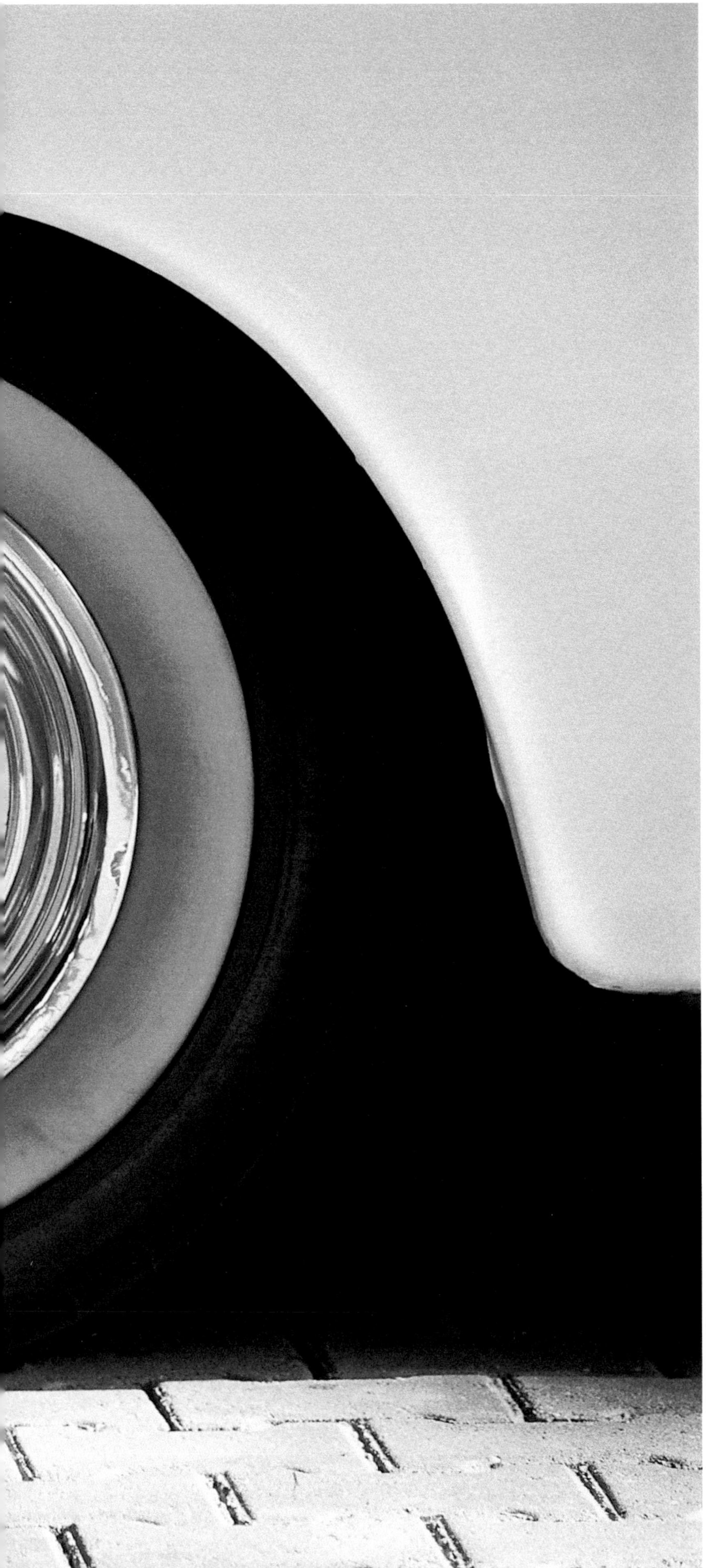

Heels and wheels

The mythical highway – Route 66

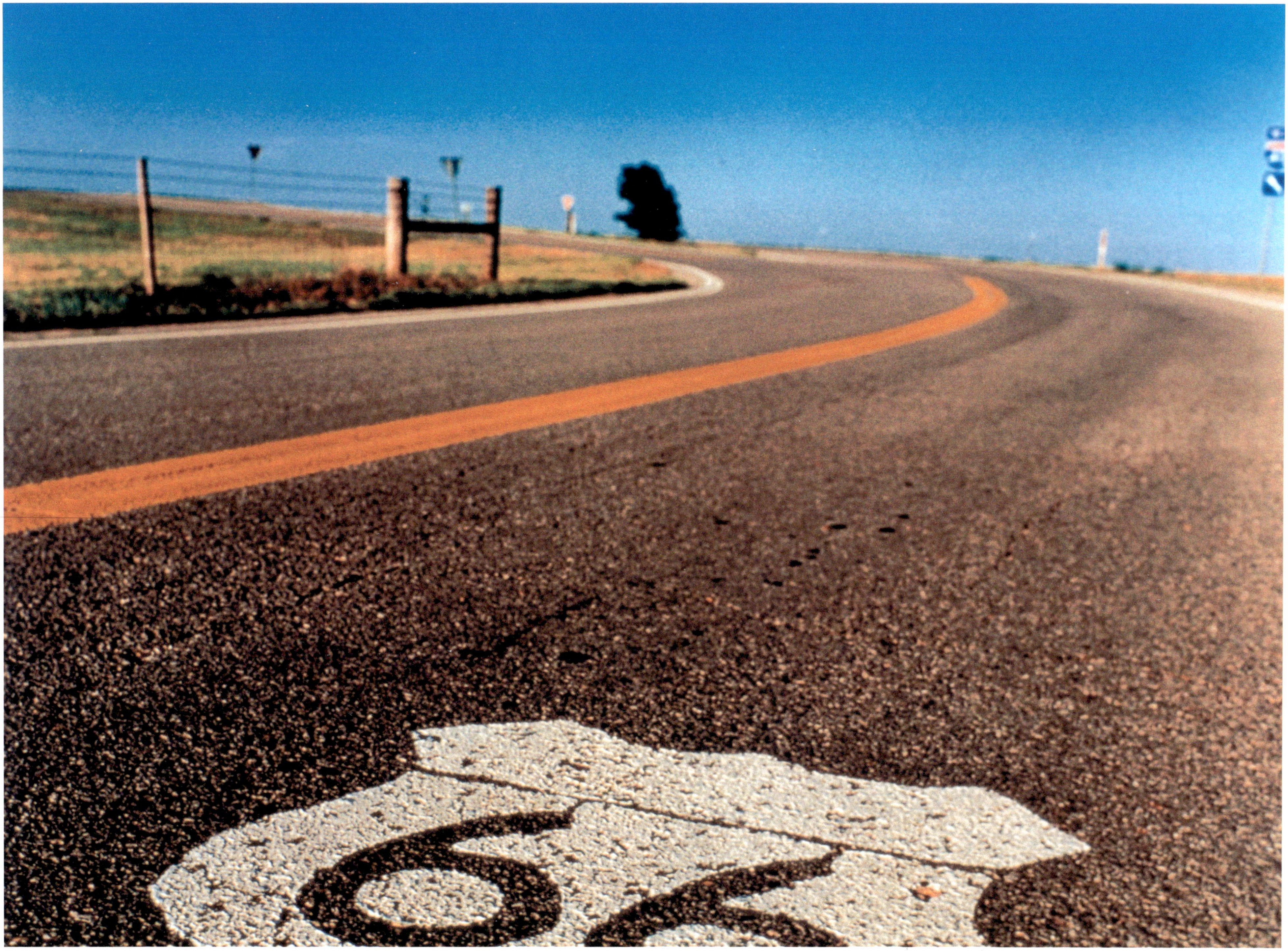

Cadillac Sixty Special Series (left) and the 1959 Cadillac Fleetwood (right)

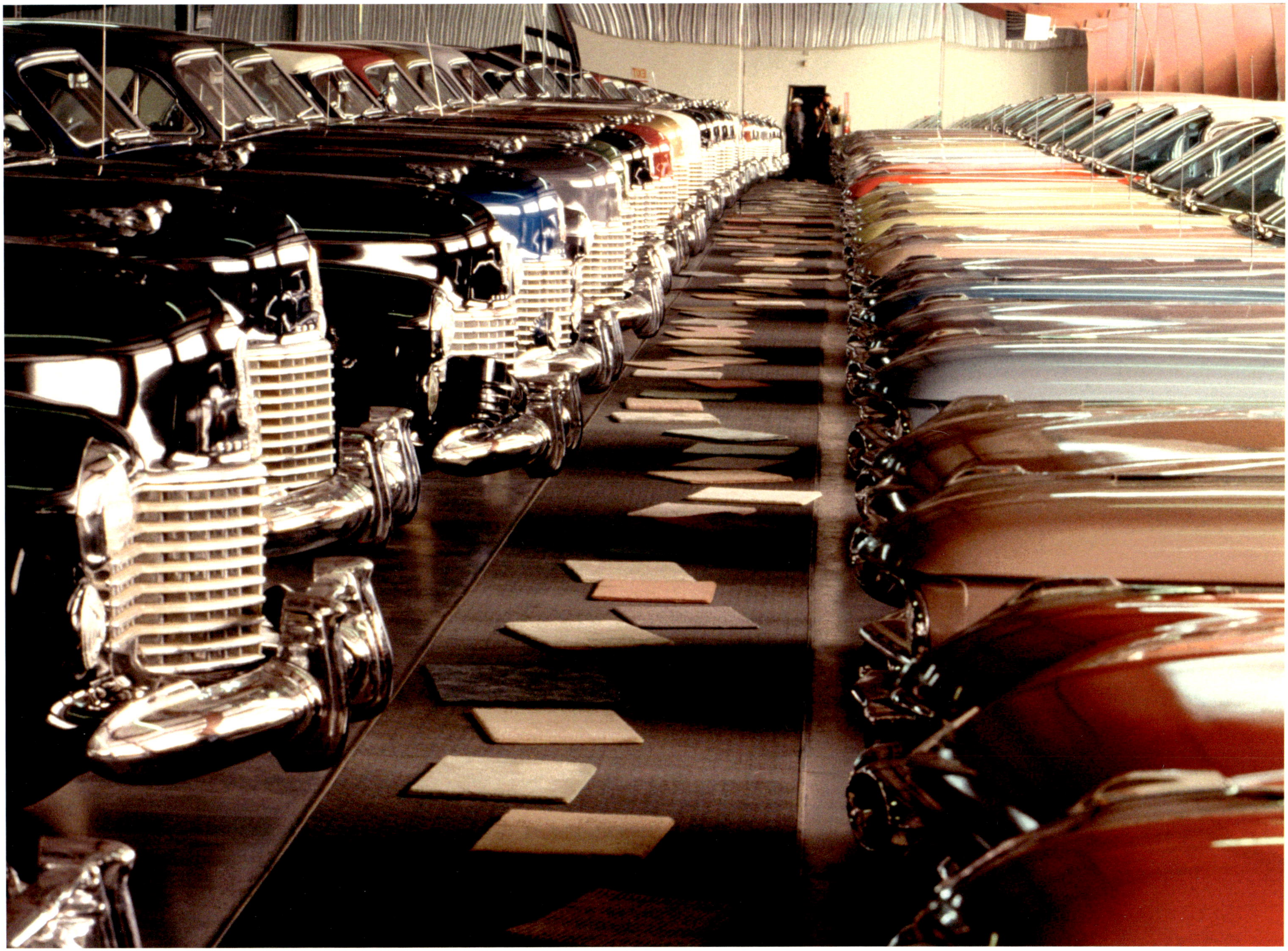

JULY 27, 1975:
ELVIS PRESLEY GAVE A GIFT OF A BRAND-NEW CADILLAC TO A BLACK BANK CLERK IN MEMPHIS. AND LEFT THE AUTO DEALER'S SHOWROOM WITH A FURTHER 13 CADILLACS FOR HIMSELF AND HIS FRIENDS.

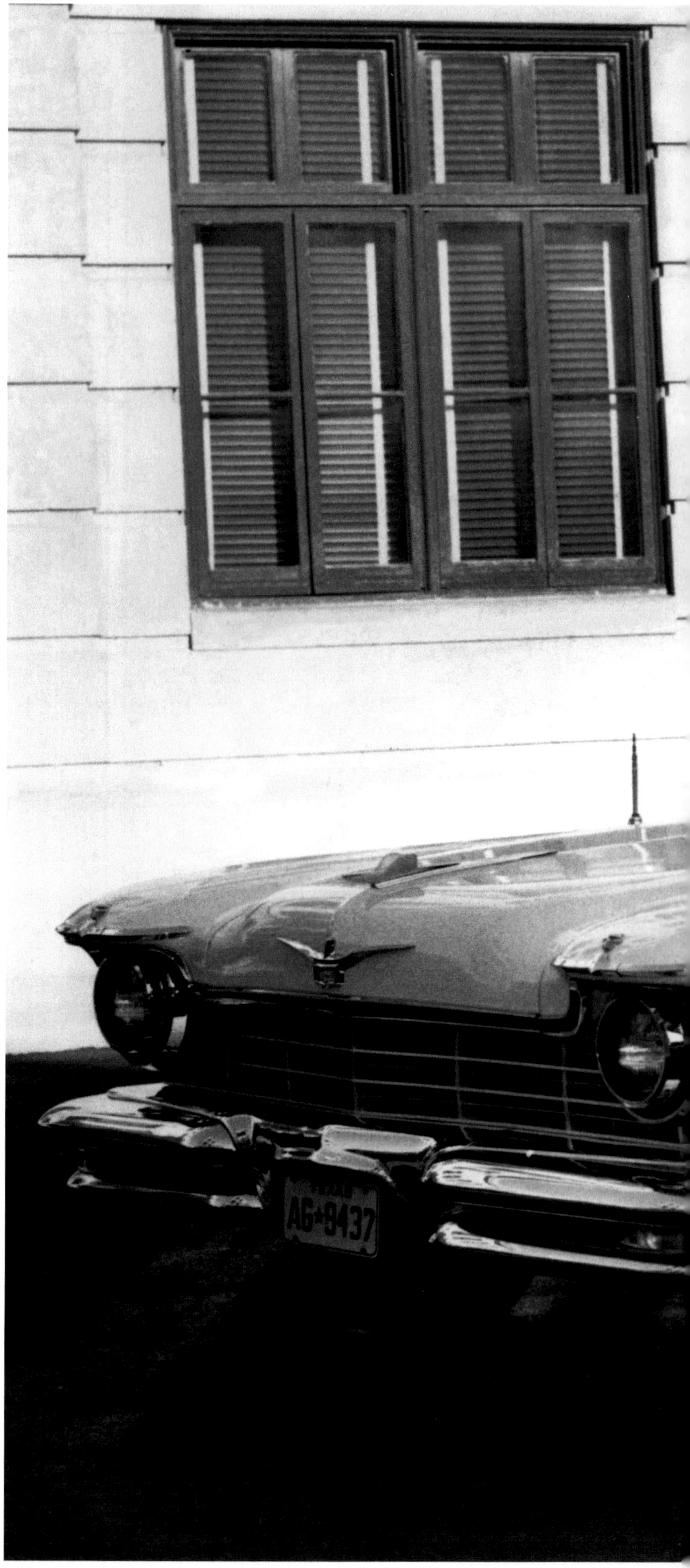

Elvis in his Cadillac Coupé in the MGM Studios, Hollywood (1958)

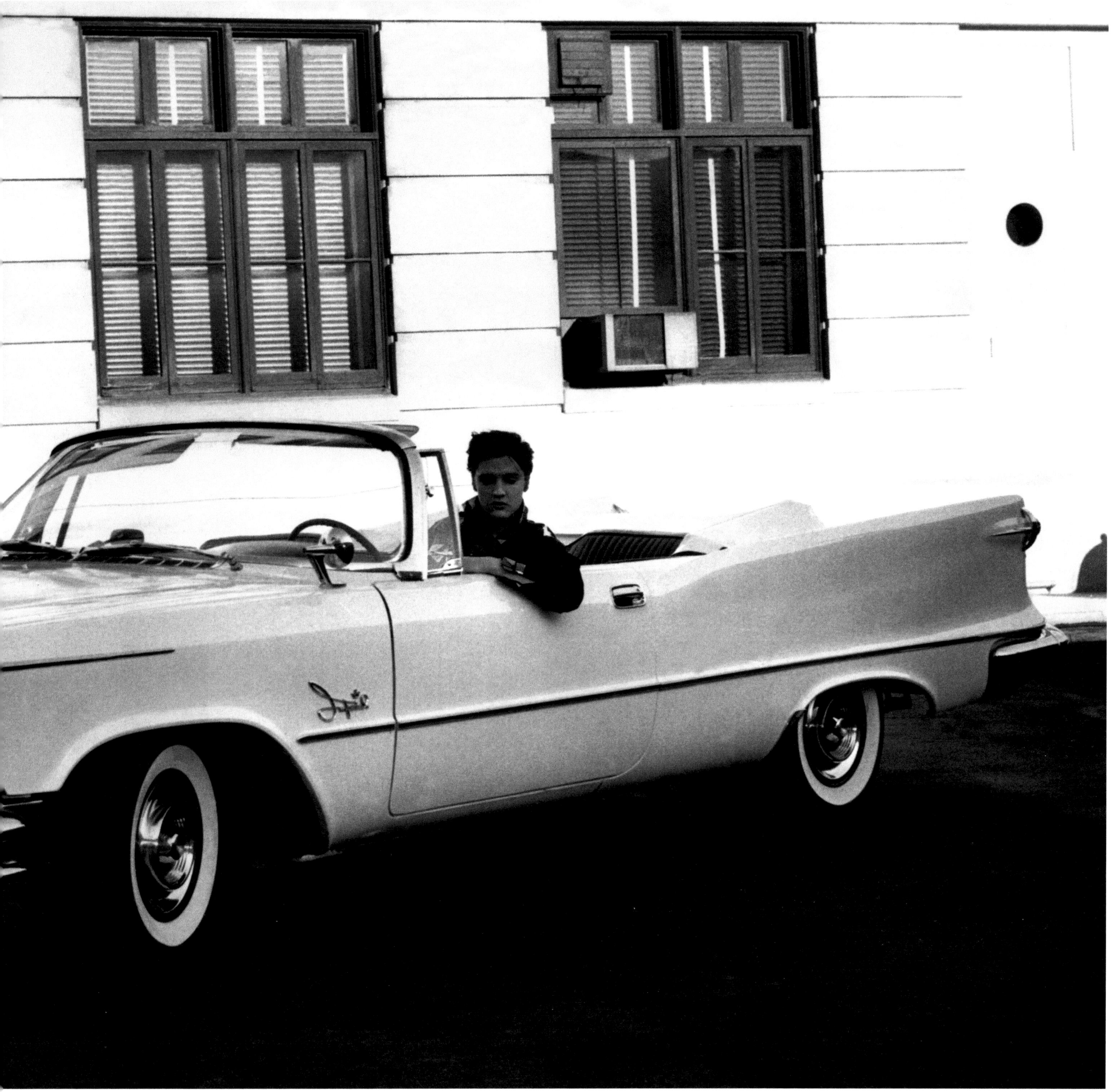

The long arm of the law drives a 1964 Dodge Polara.

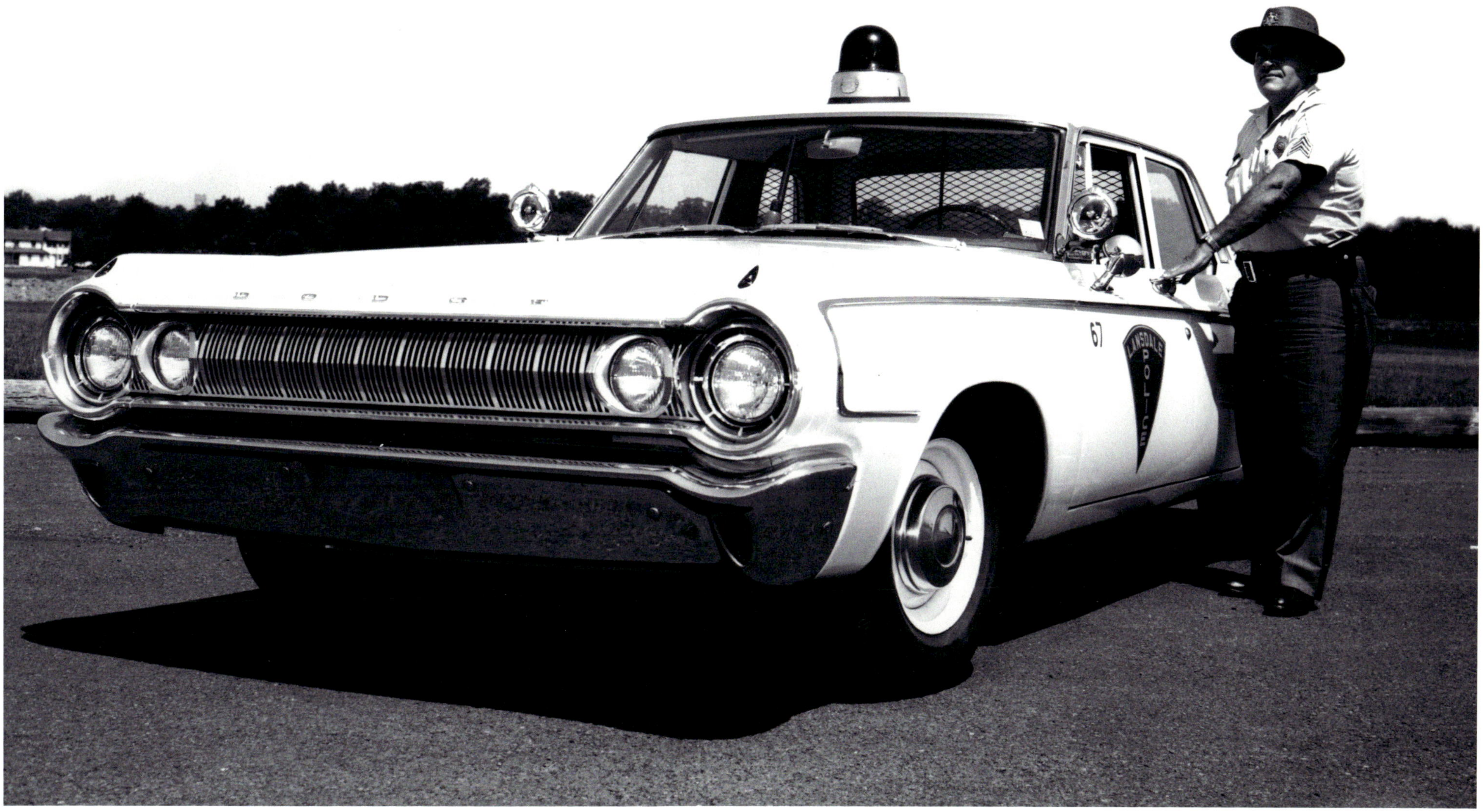

67
LANSDALE
POLICE

1963 Pontiac Catalina

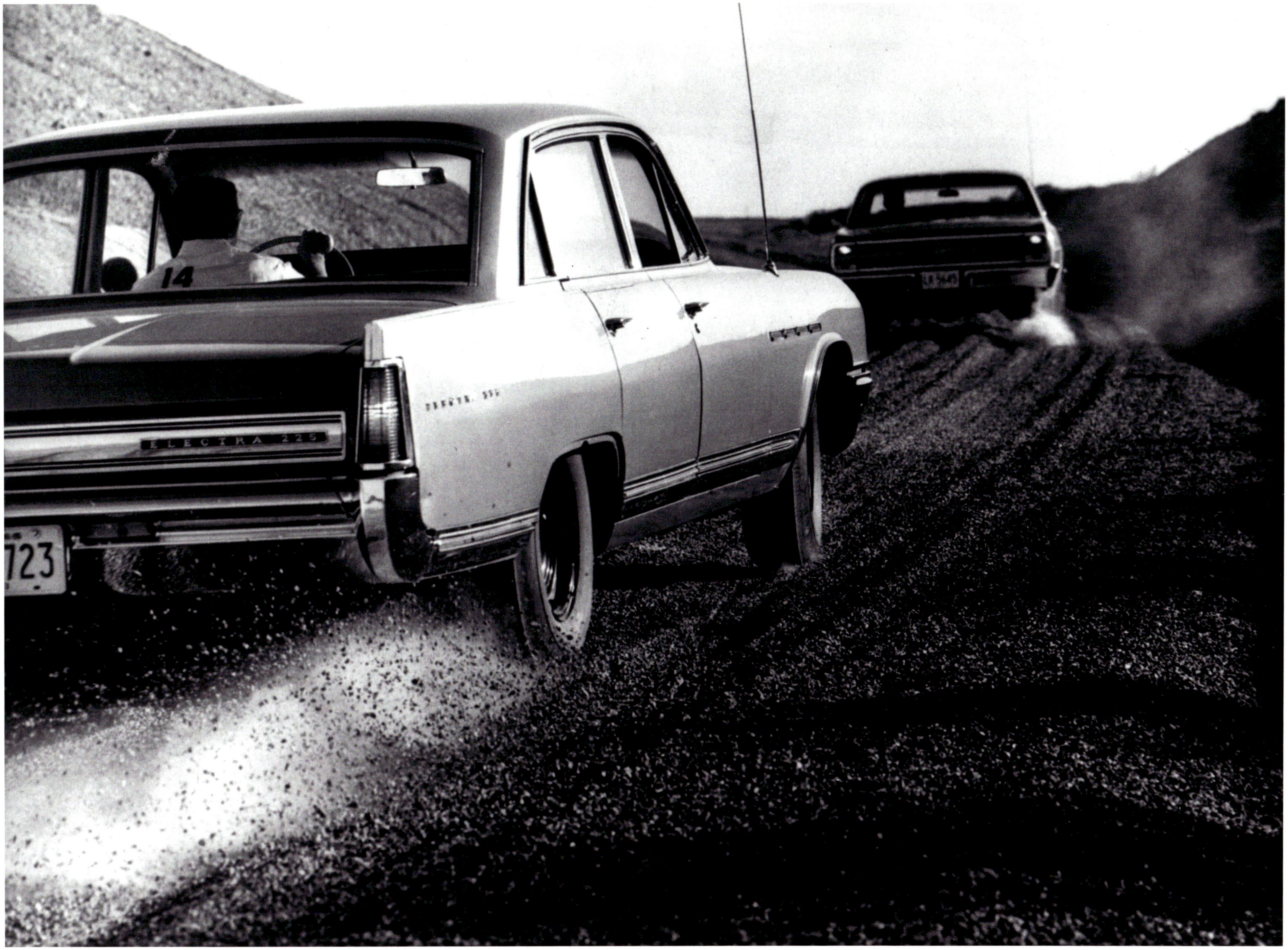
14
ELECTRA 225

THE FREEWAY –
SYNONYM FOR FREEDOM.

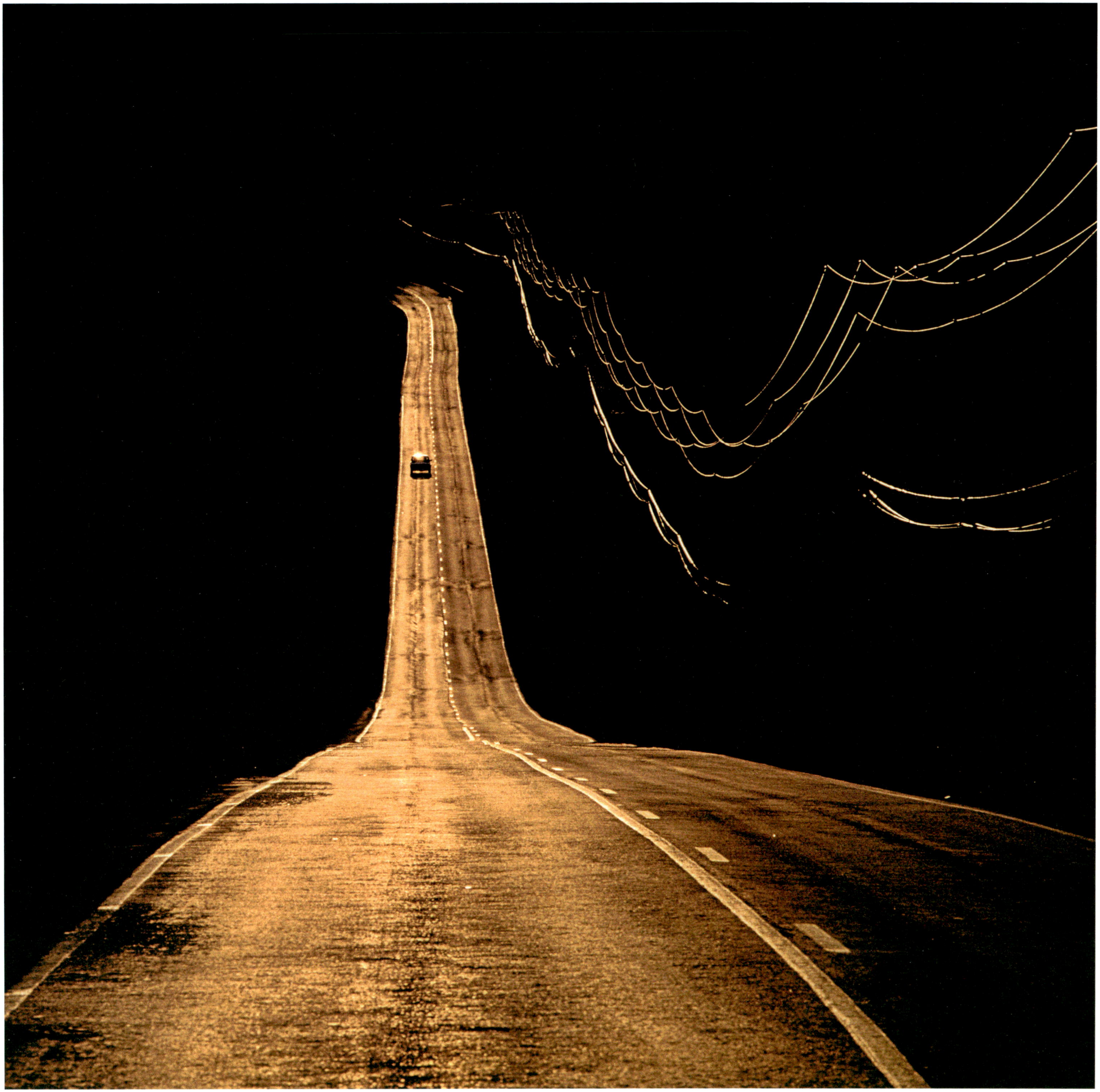

1955 Chevrolet Bel Air Nomad

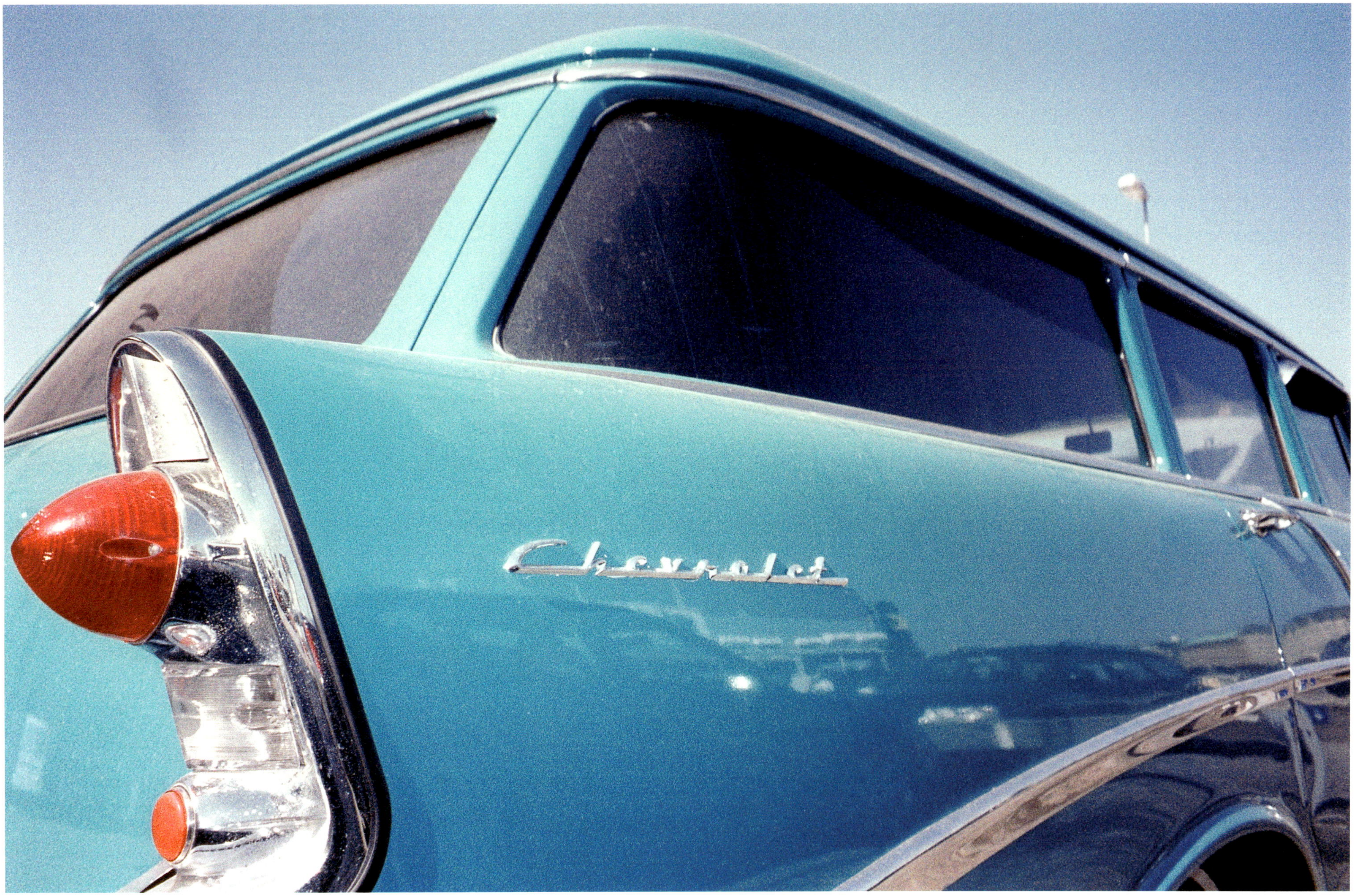
Chevrolet

1957 Buick Special

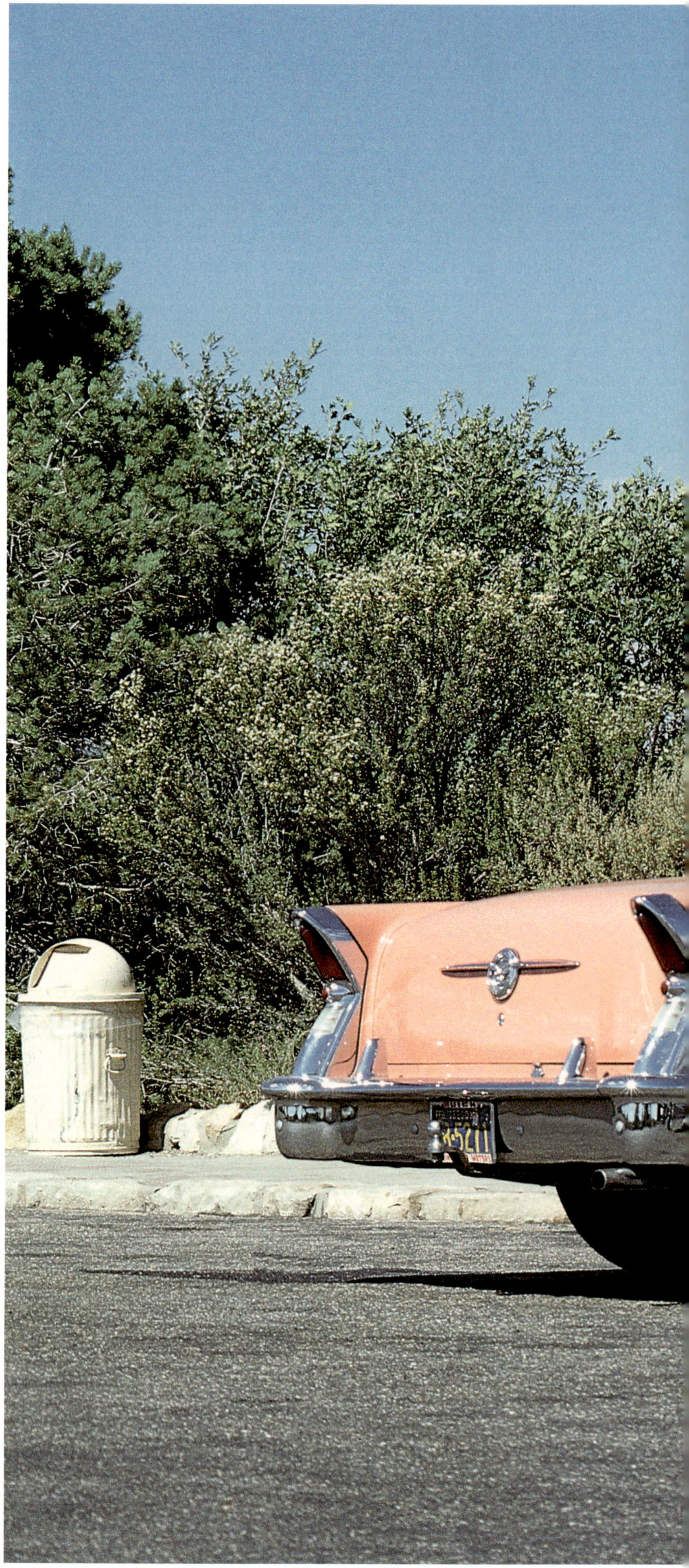

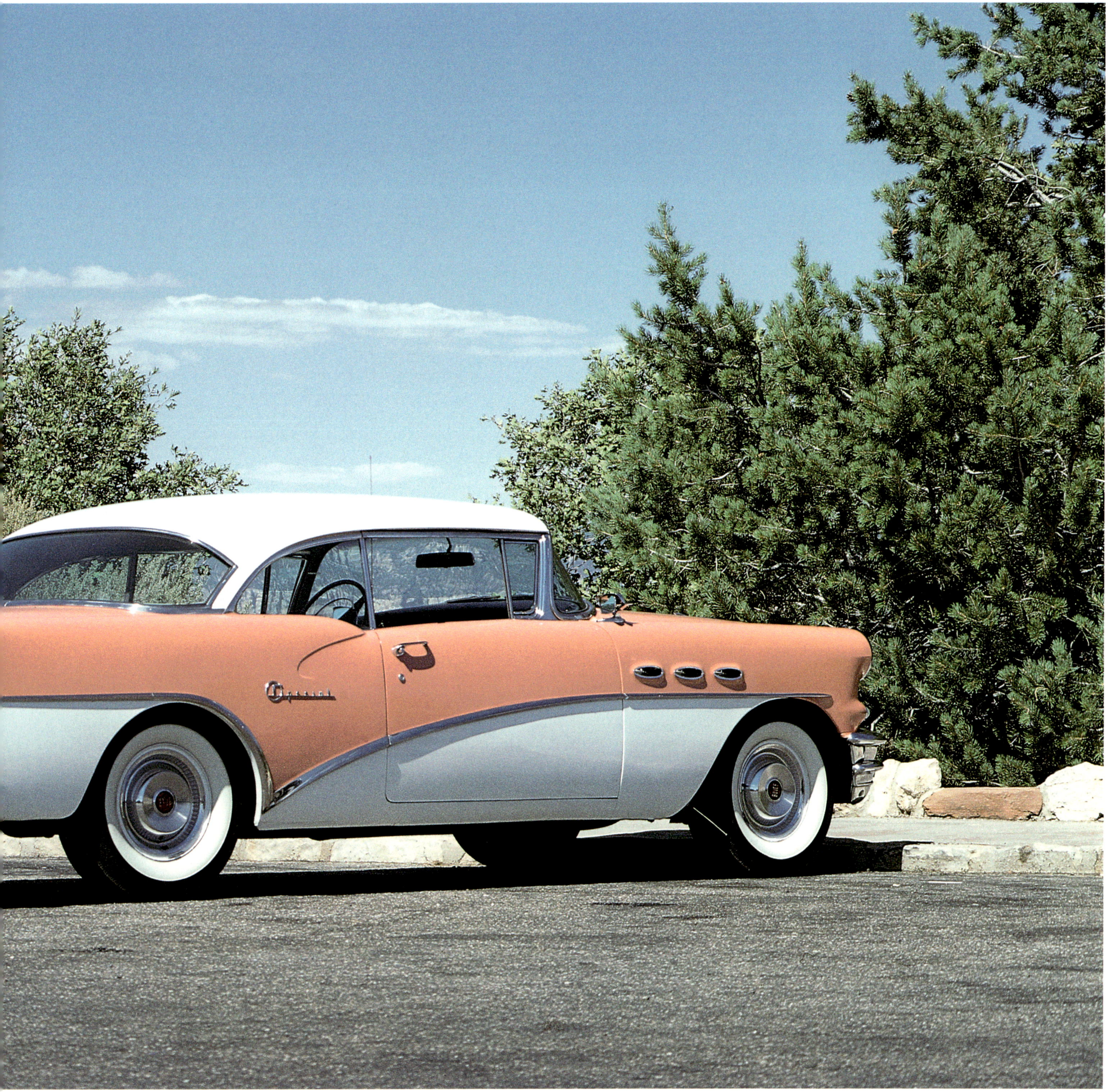

WE ALWAYS TAKE MY CAR
CAUSE IT'S NEVER BEEN BEAT
AND WE'VE NEVER MISSED YET
WITH THE GIRLS WE MEET
NONE OF THE GUYS GO STEADY
CAUSE IT WOULDN'T BE RIGHT
TO LEAVE THEIR BEST GIRL HOME
NOW ON SATURDAY NIGHT

BEACH BOYS – "I GET AROUND"

The radio – the most important interior detail

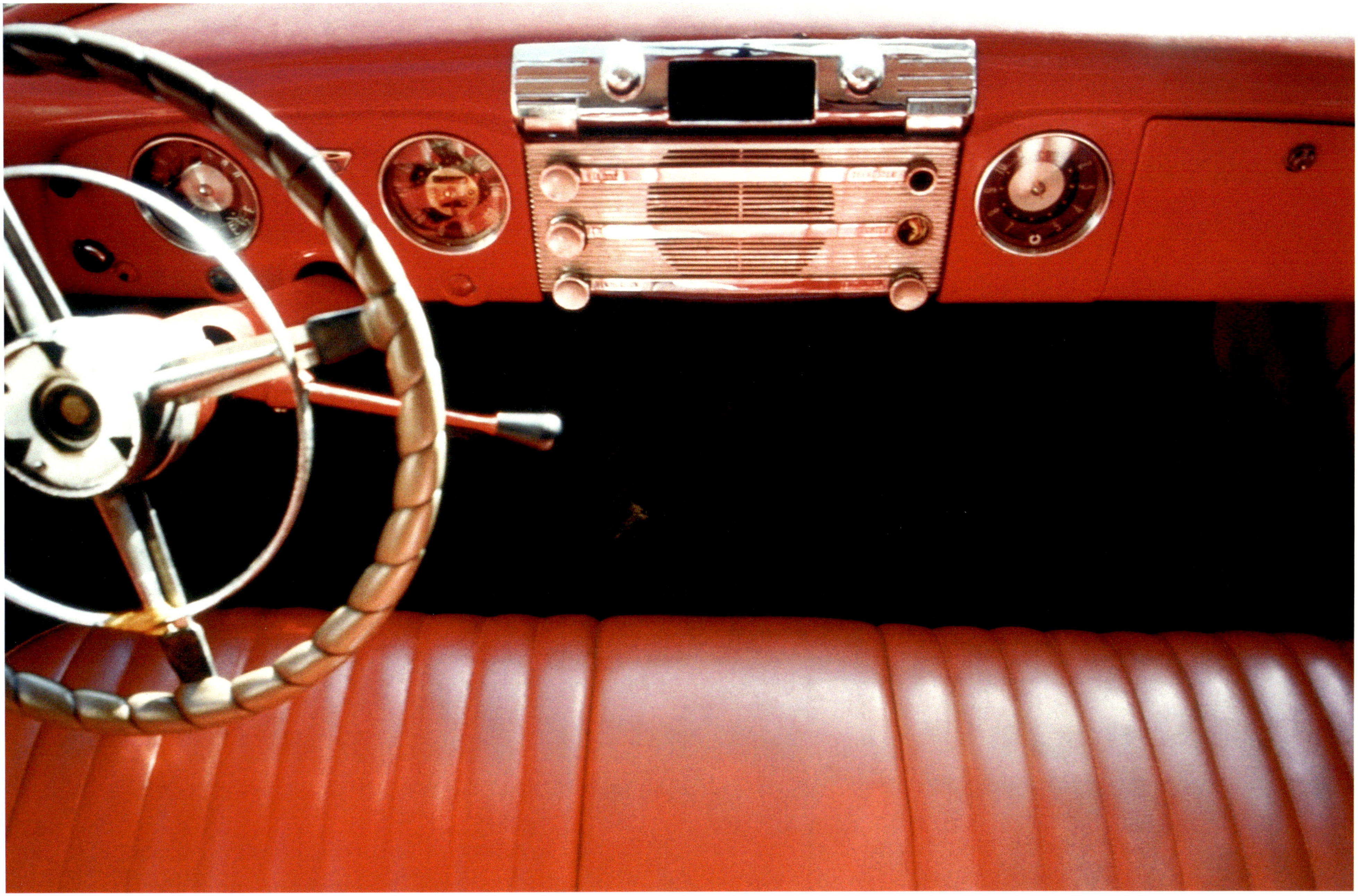

1958 Packard

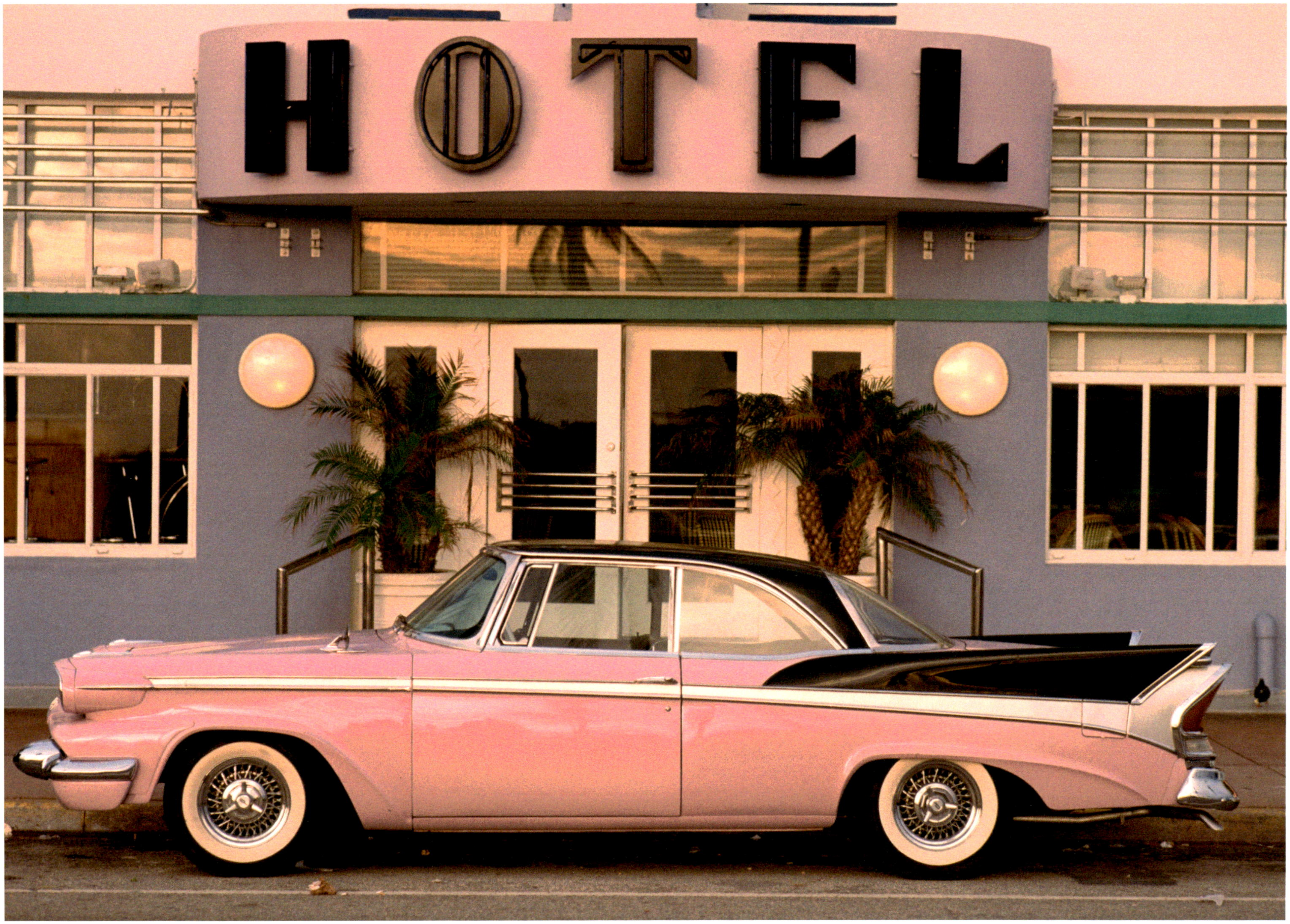
HOTEL

**EVERYTIME I HAVE A DATE
THERE'S ONLY ONE PLACE TO GO
THAT'S TO THE DRIVE IN
IT'S SUCH A GROOVY PLACE TO TALK
AND MAYBE WATCH A SHOW
DOWN AT THE DRIVE IN**

THE BEACH BOYS – "DRIVE-IN"

Drive-In: because, after all, drivers too need to refuel.

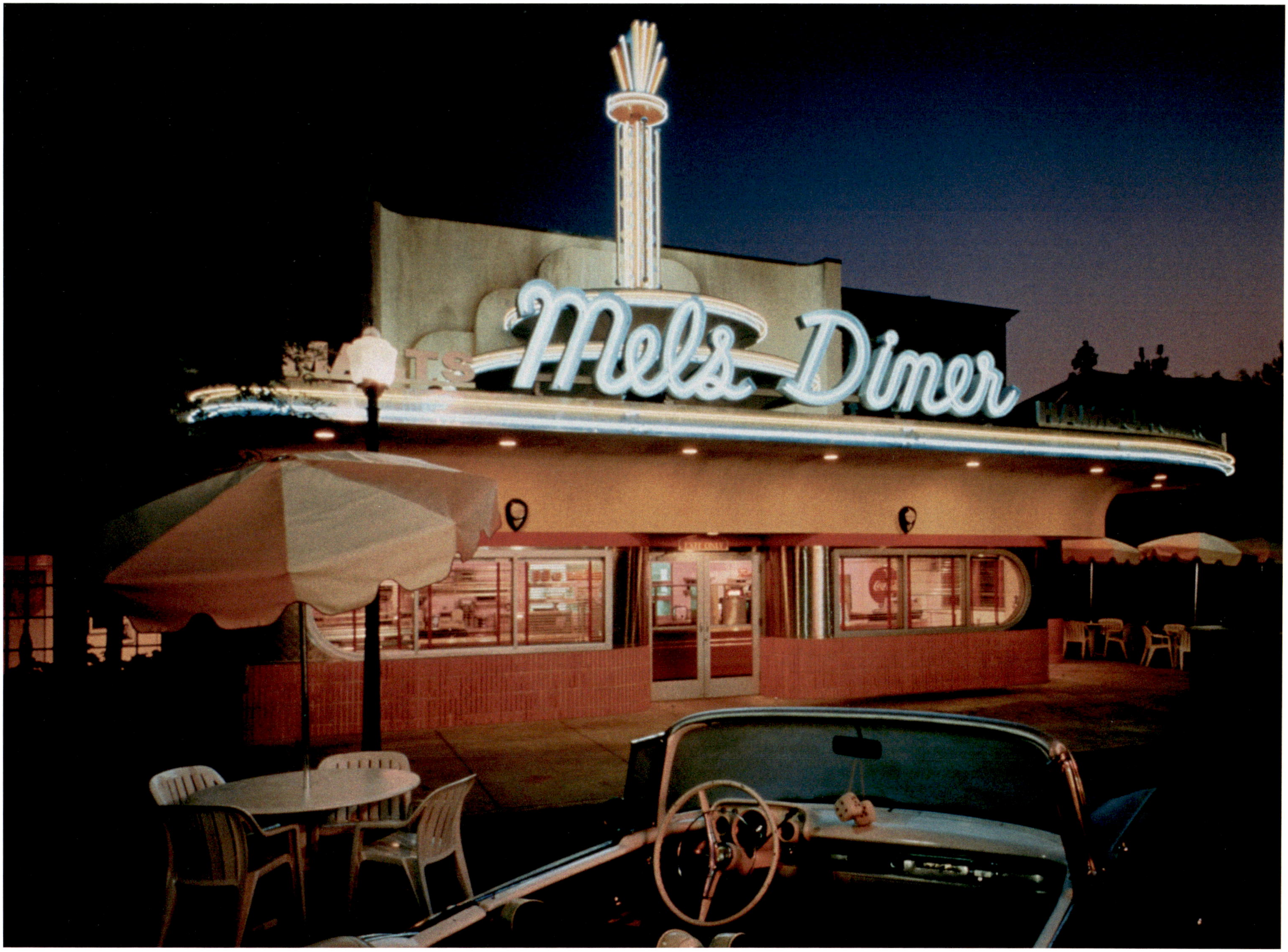
Mels Diner

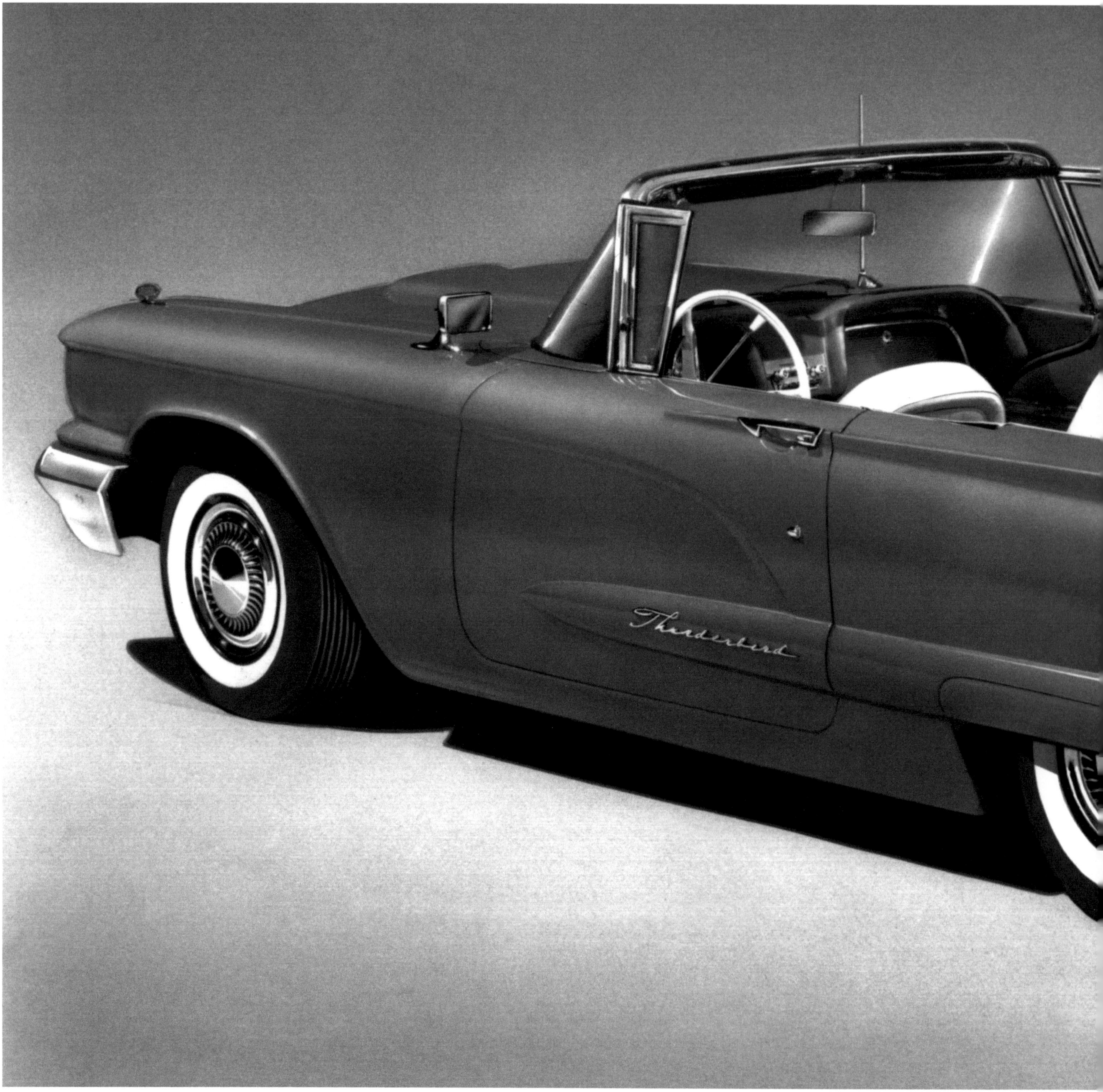
Thunderbird

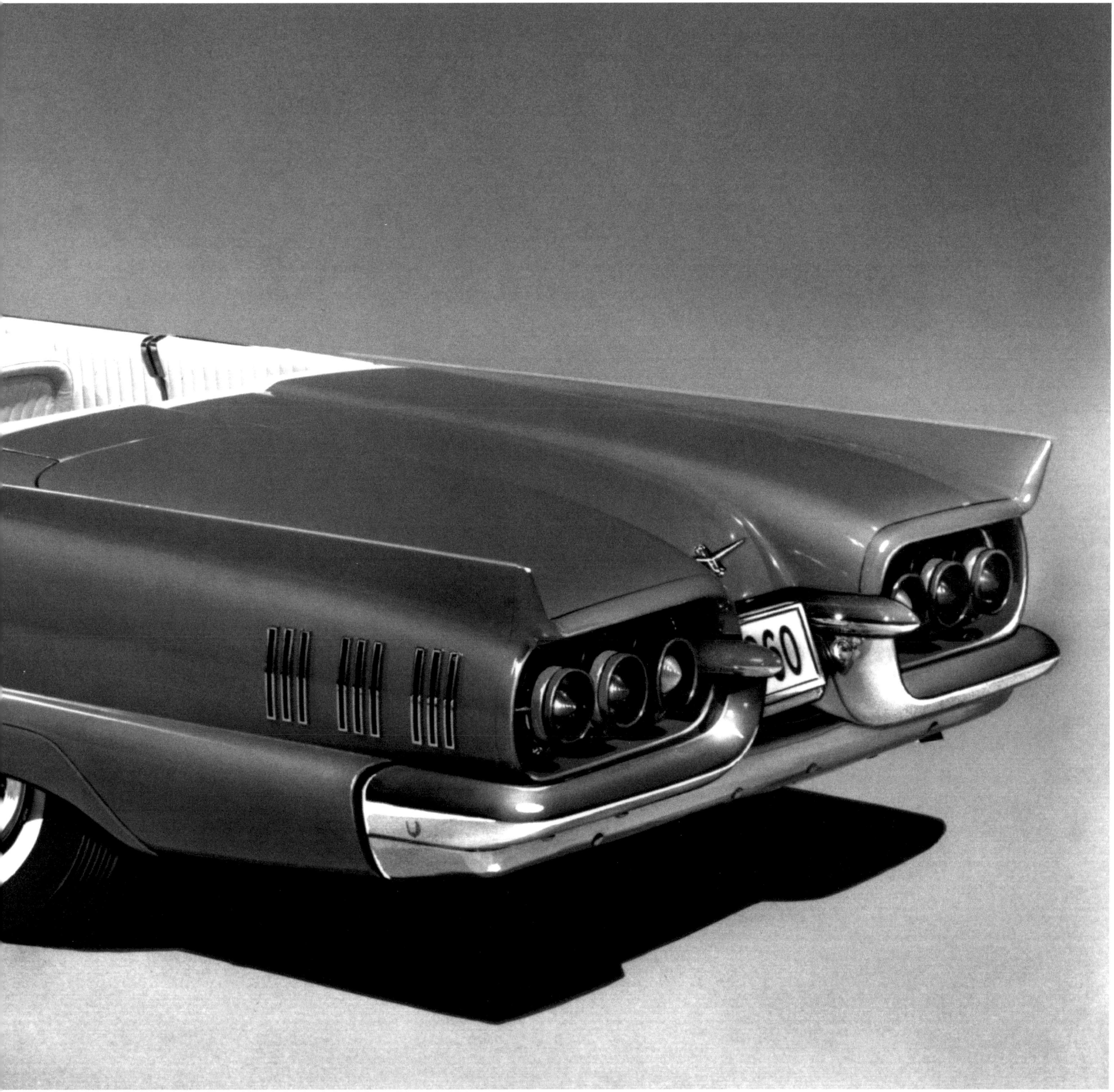

YOU BUY A CAR.
AND YOU GET A LIFESTYLE.

1960 Ford Thunderbird (previous page)
1961 Cadillac Fleetwood

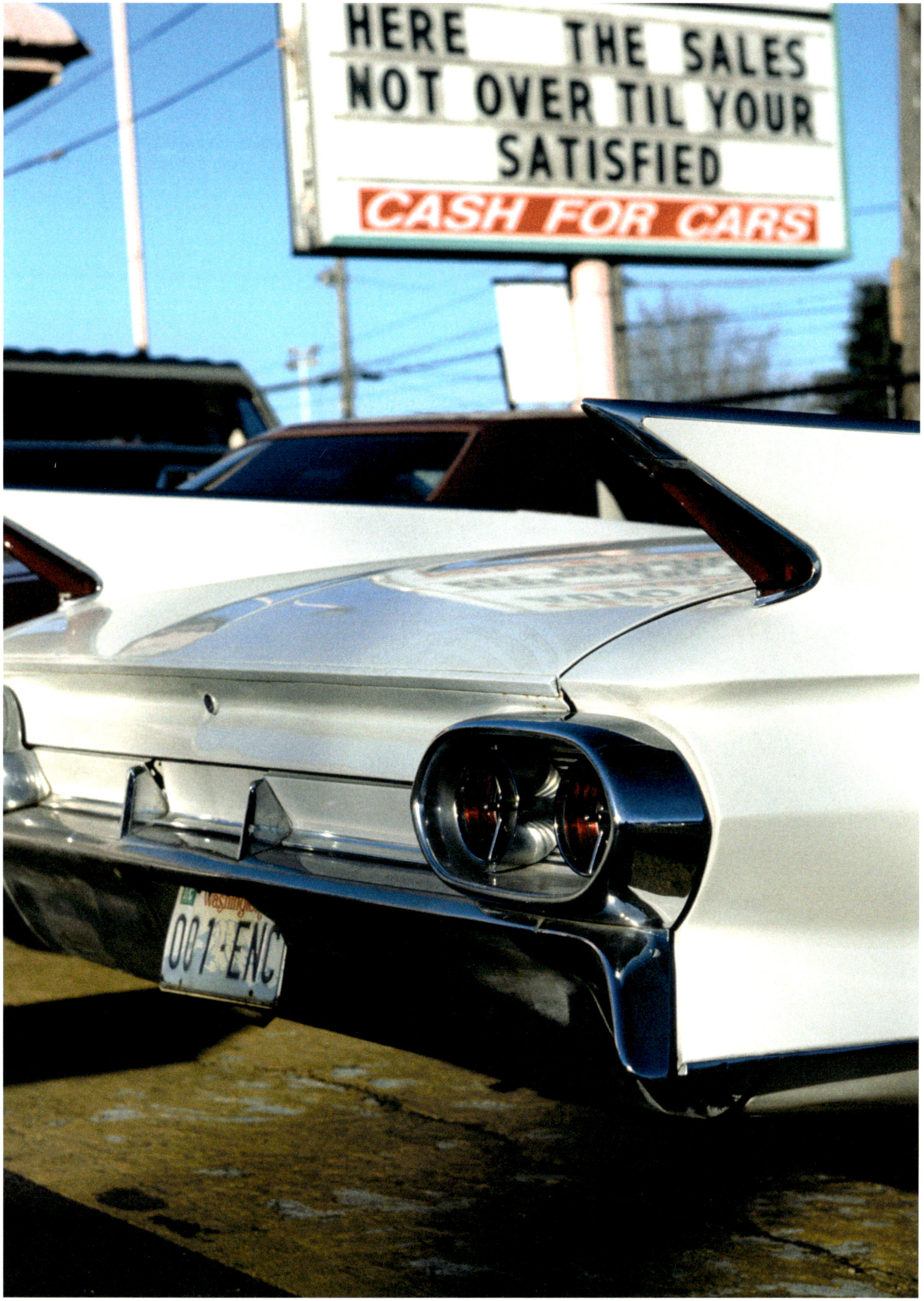
HERE THE SALES
NOT OVER TIL YOUR
SATISFIED
CASH FOR CARS
001 ENC

NO CAR – NO GIRL.

Hanging out during the Rockabilly Weekender Car Show
(April 20, 2000 Las Vegas, Nevada)

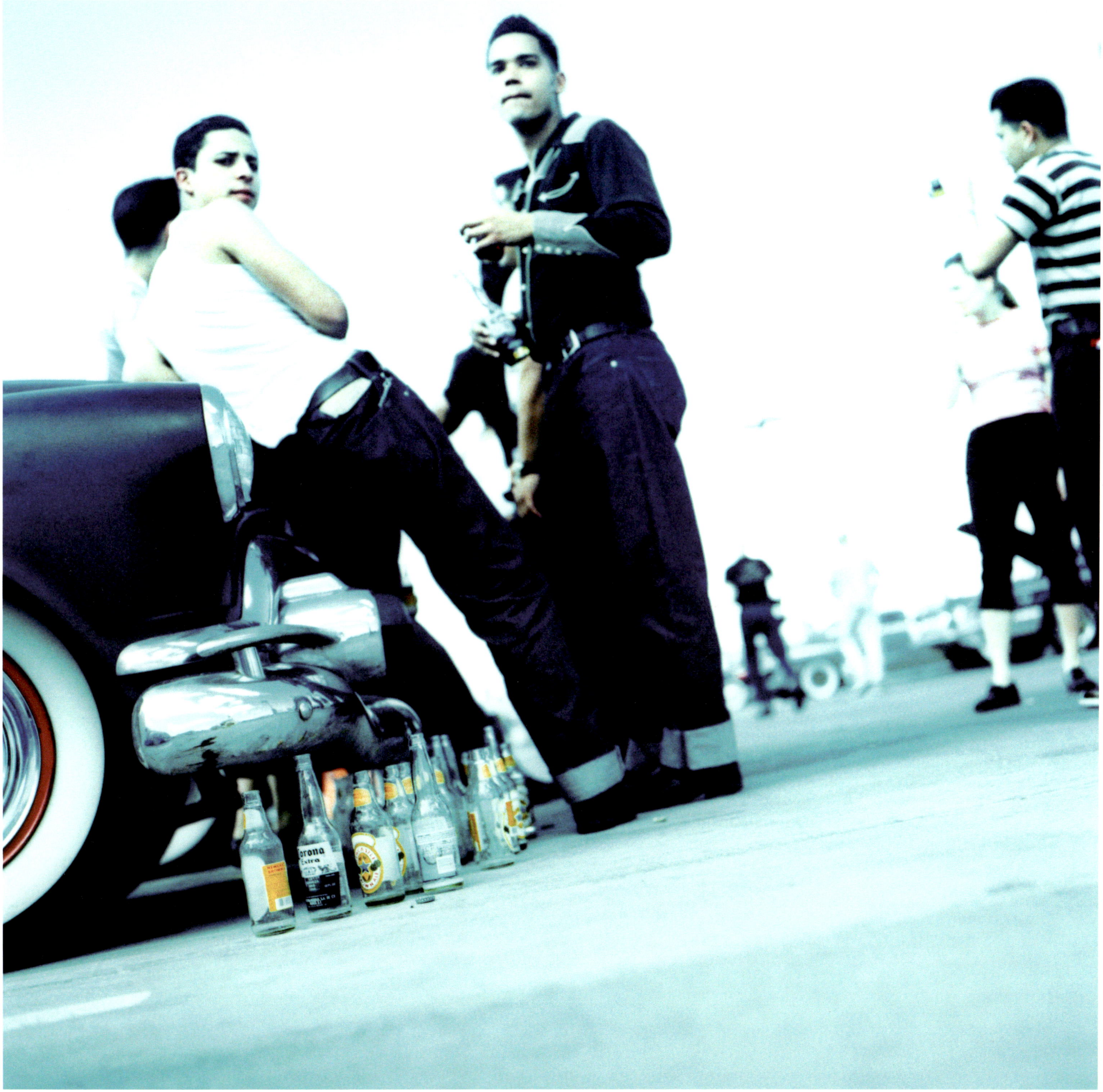
Corona Extra

1960 Ford Thunderbird

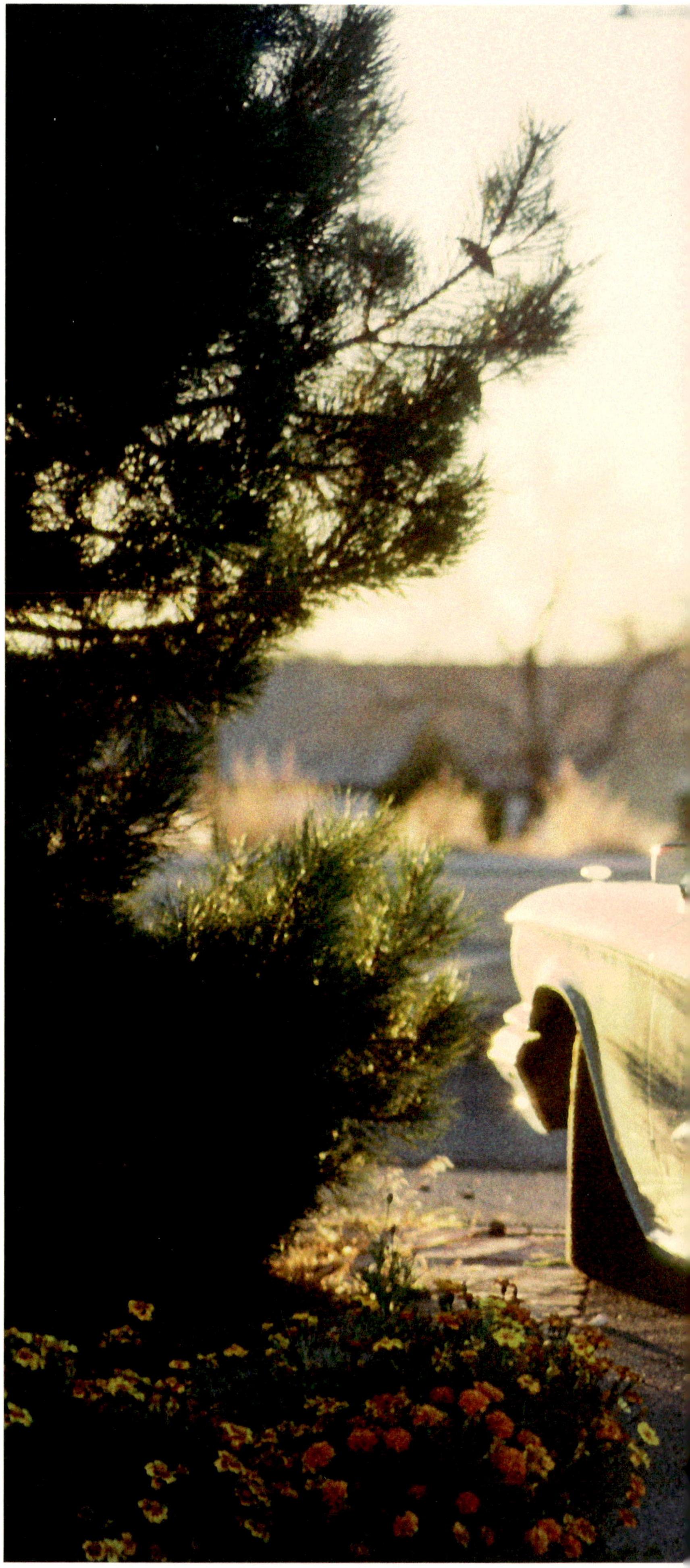

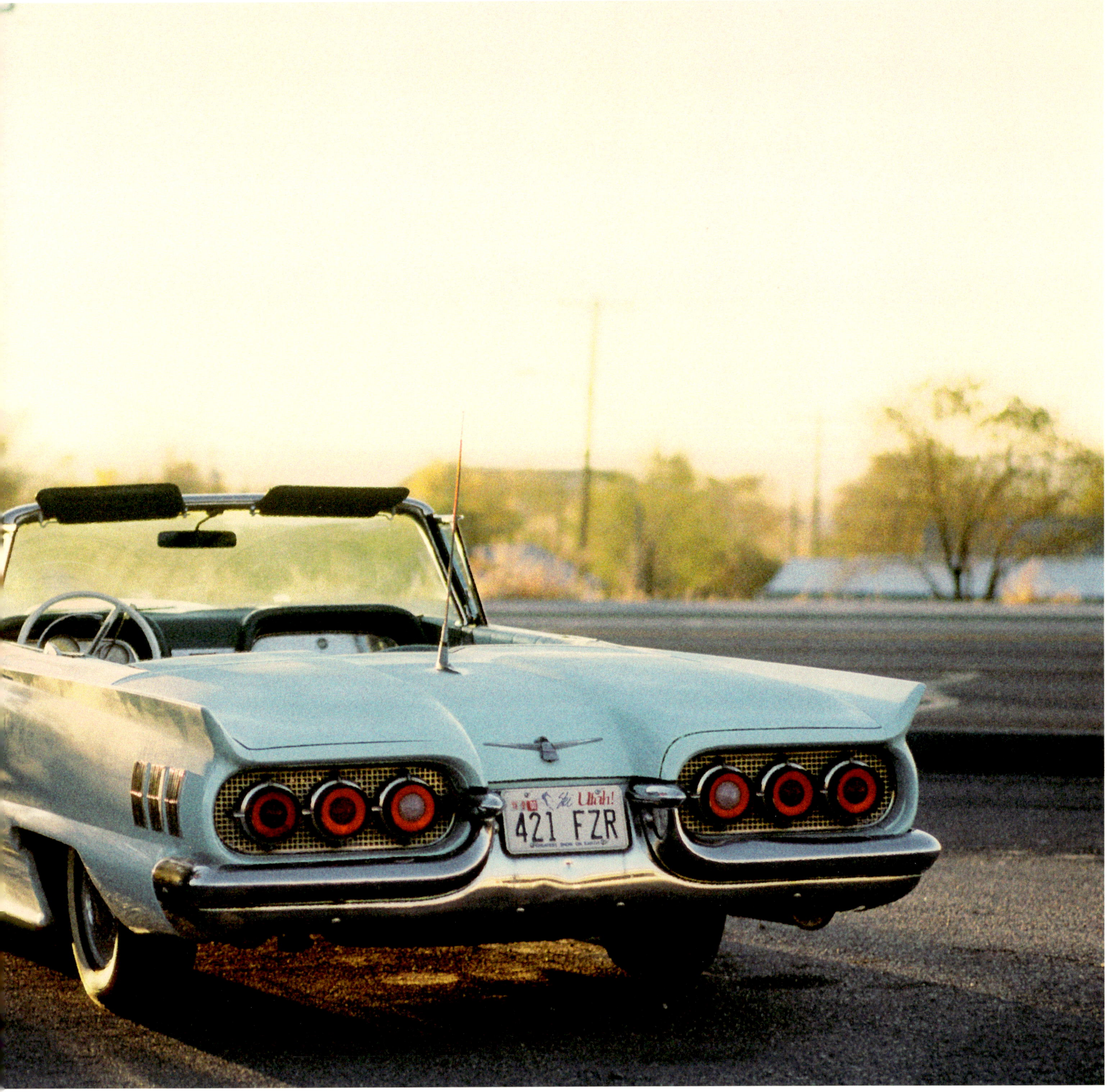
Utah!
421 FZR

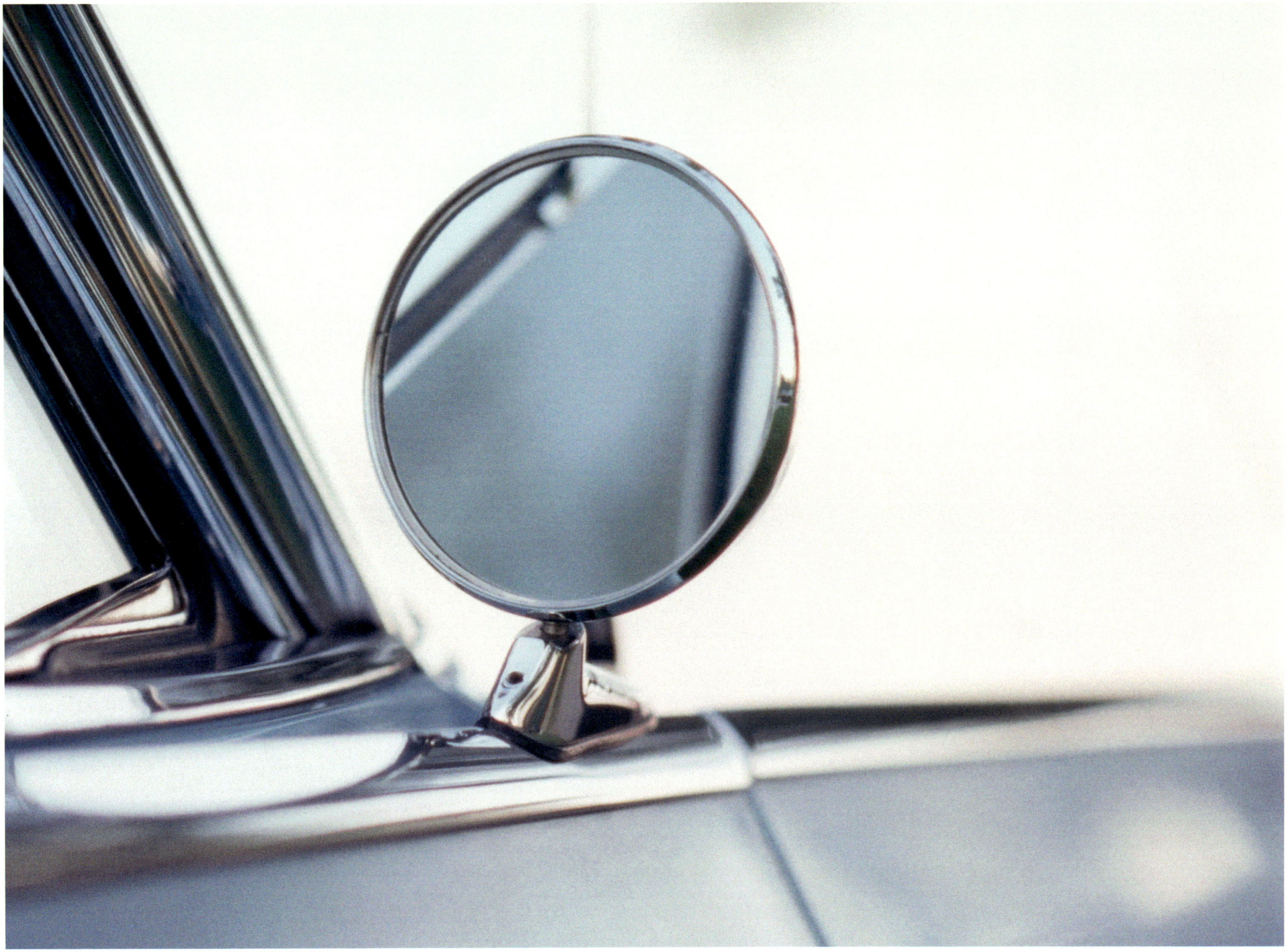

1962 Ford Thunderbird

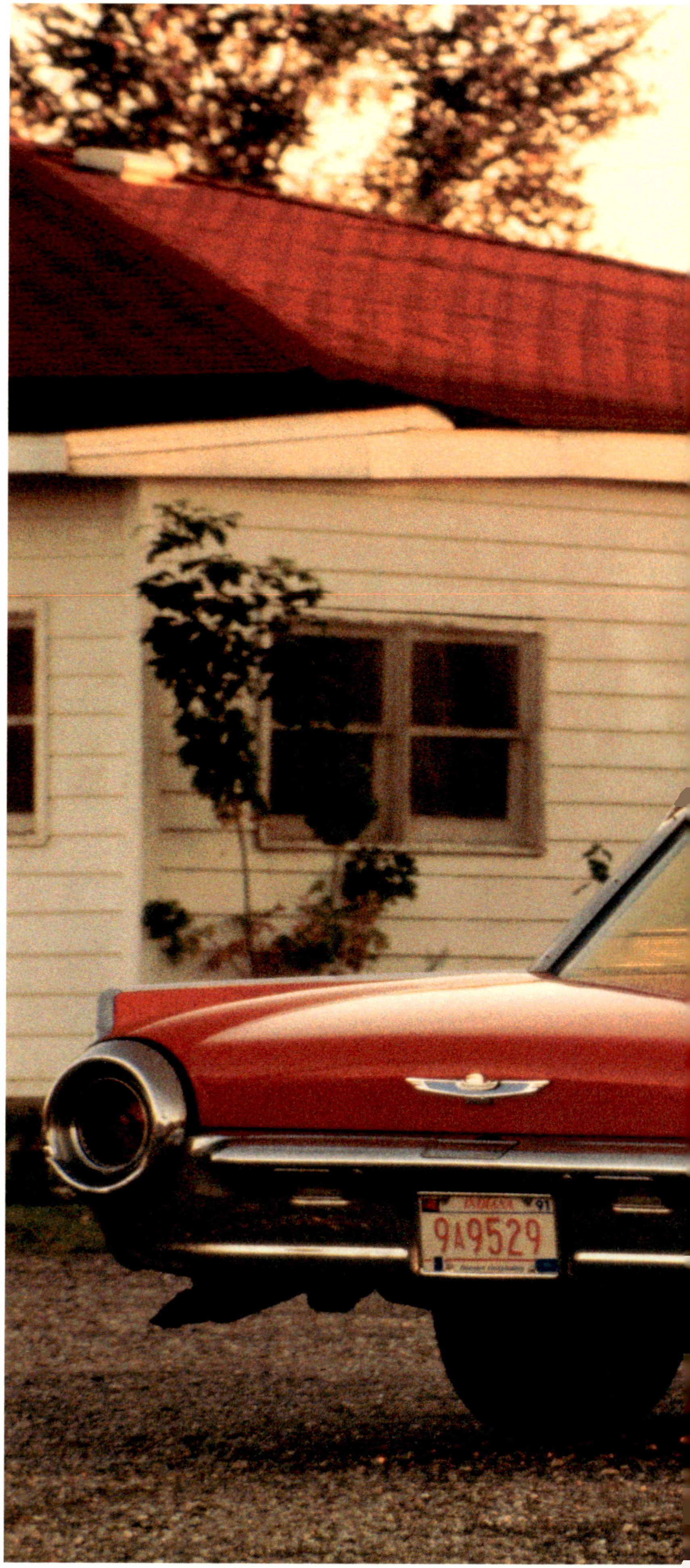

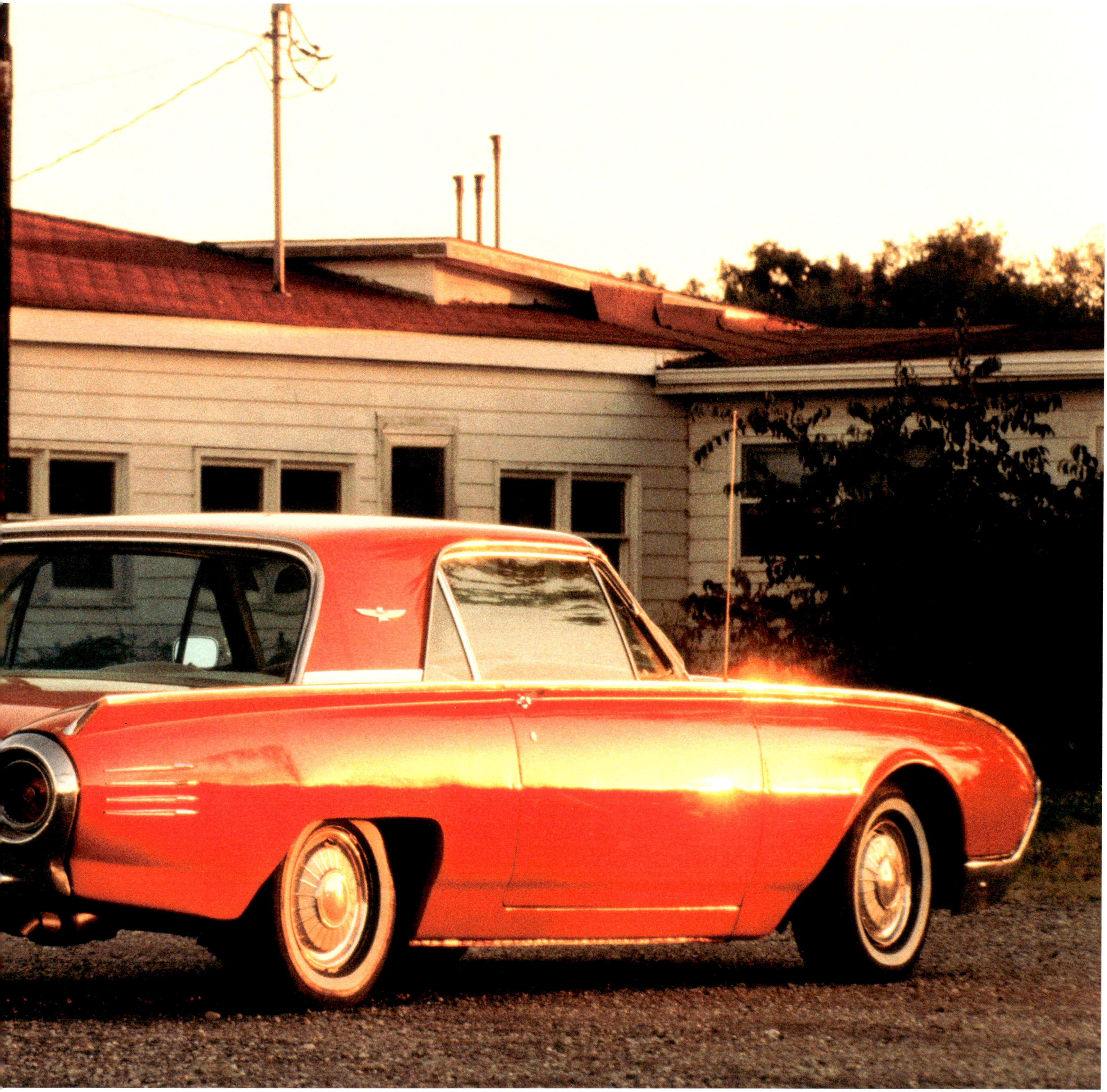

**DRIVING – JUST DRIVING.
NOT TO ARRIVE ANYWHERE, BUT TO BE
ON THE ROAD.**

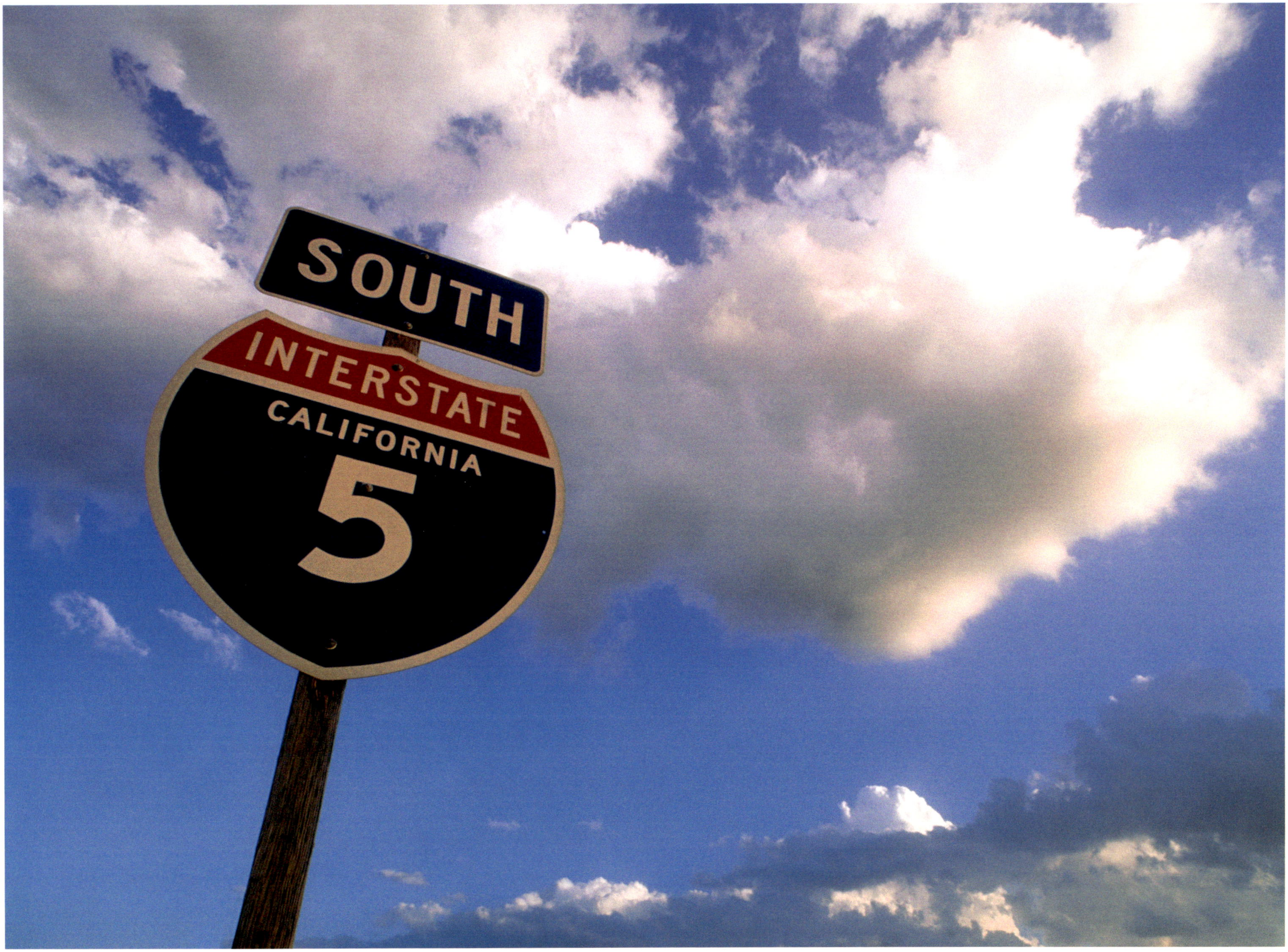
SOUTH
INTERSTATE
CALIFORNIA
5

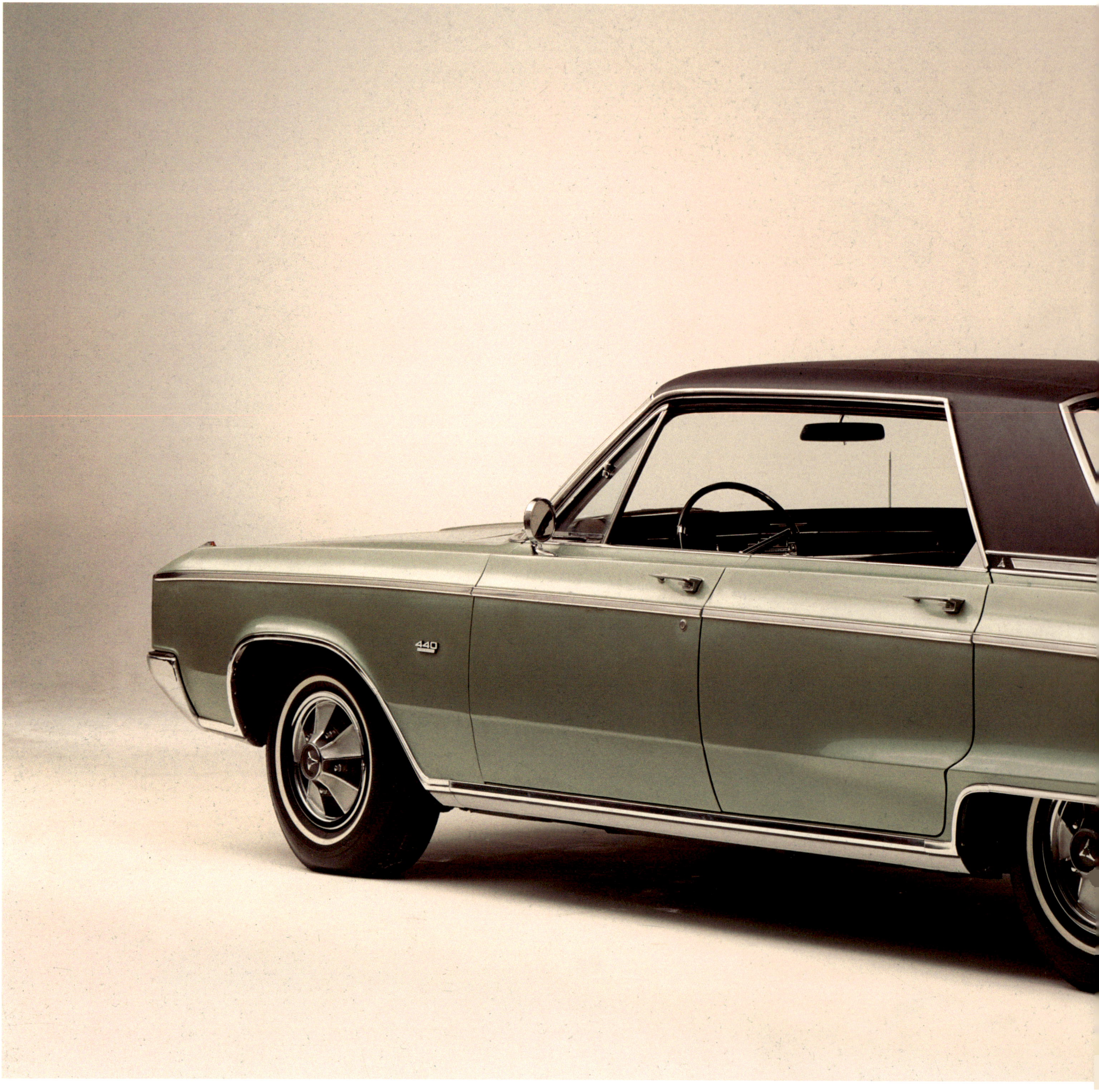
440

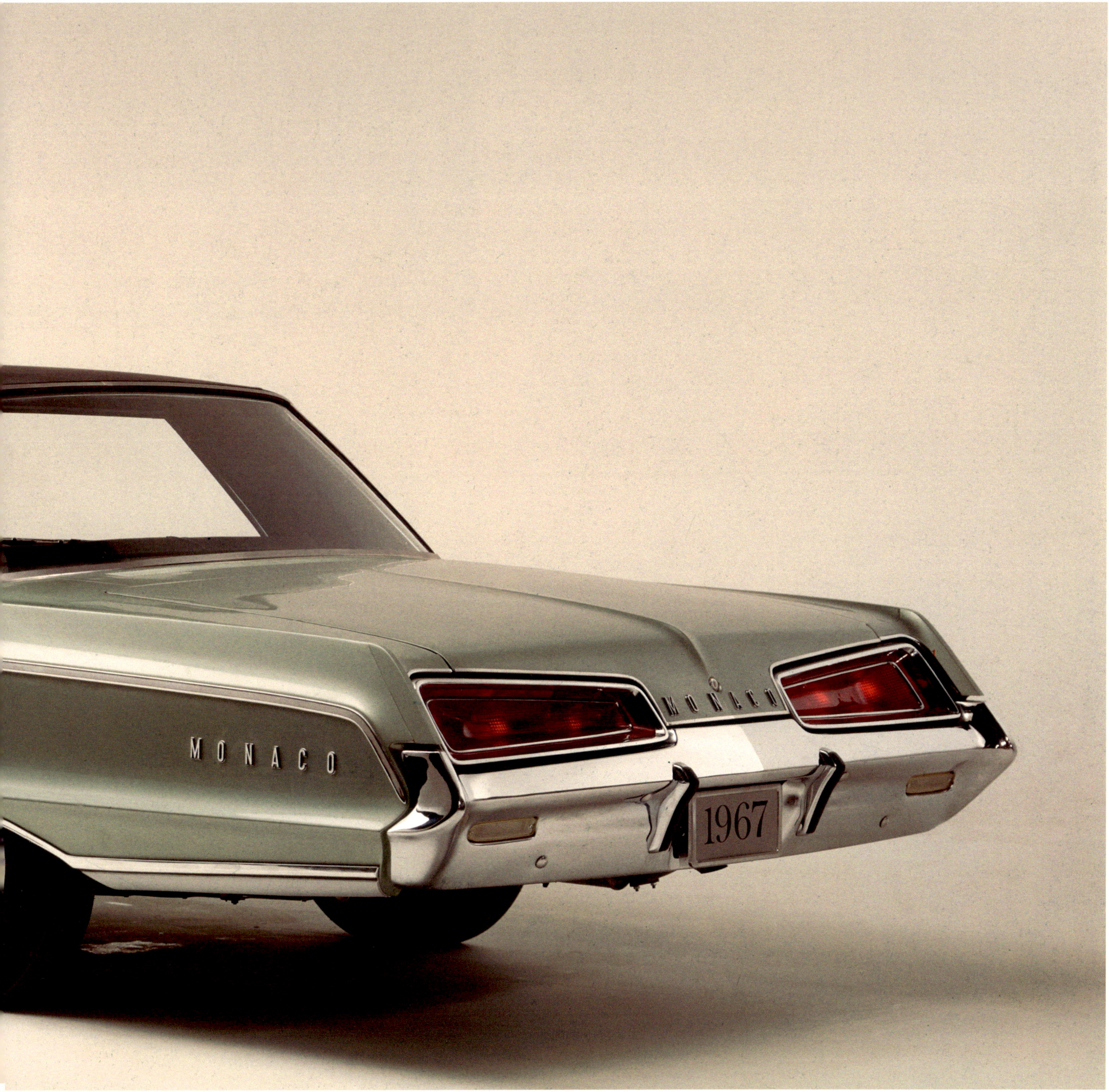
MONACO
1967

1967 Dodge Monaco (previous page)
1958 Chevrolet Corvette

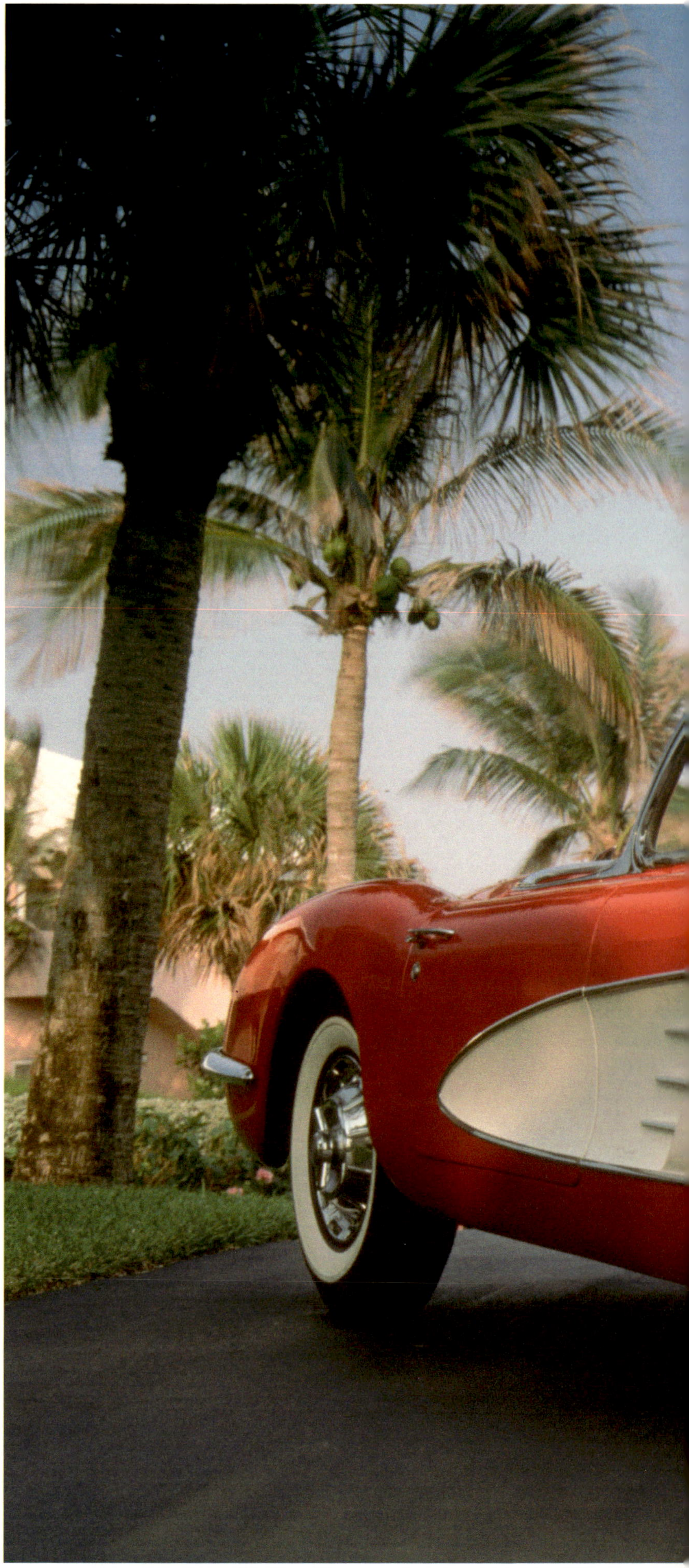

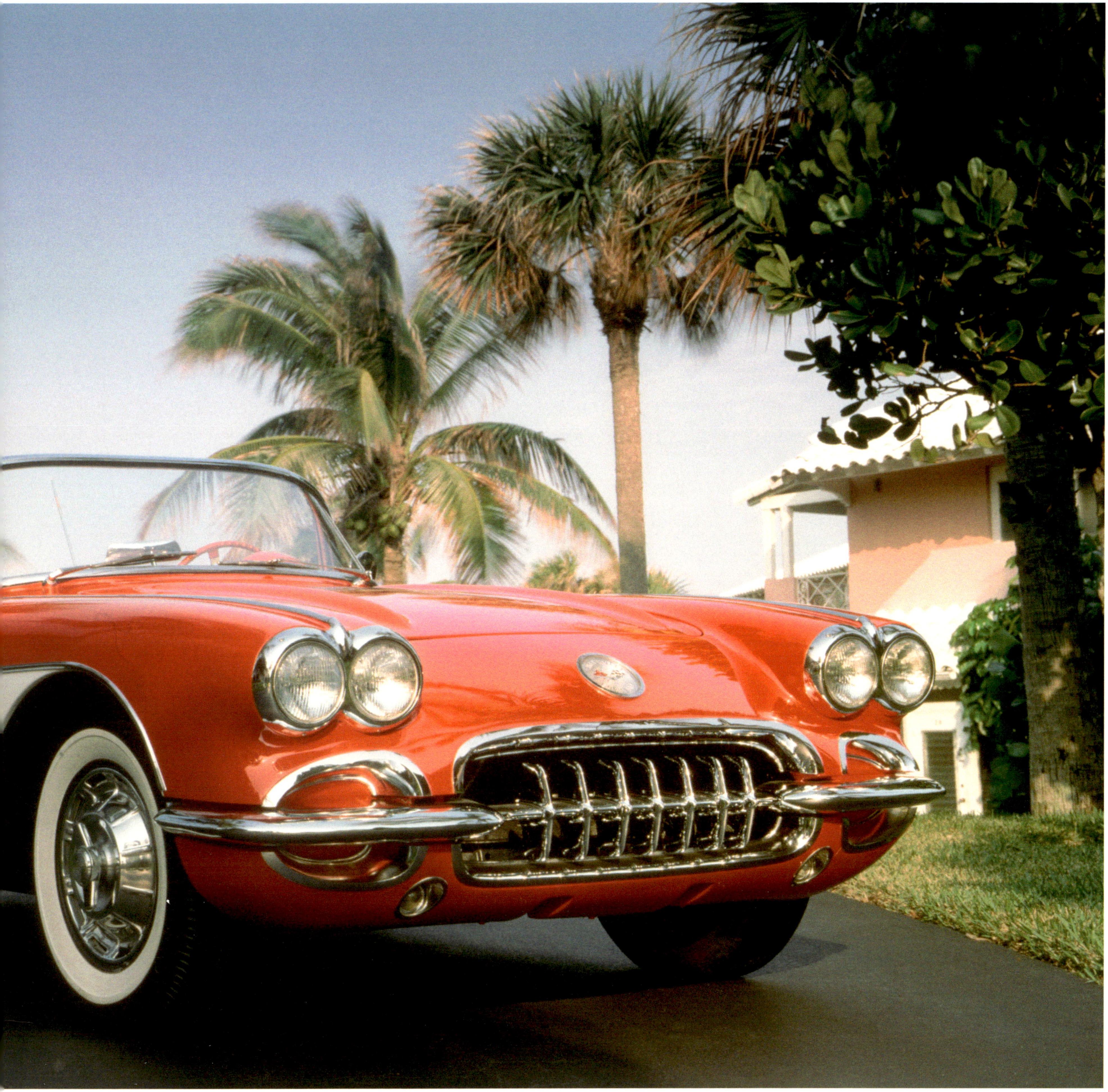

HIGH TAILFINS –
INSPIRED BY AIRPLANE DESIGN, CAR TAILFINS IN THE FIFTIES SEEMED TO GET EVER LONGER AND HIGHER.

1961 Cadillac Fleetwood

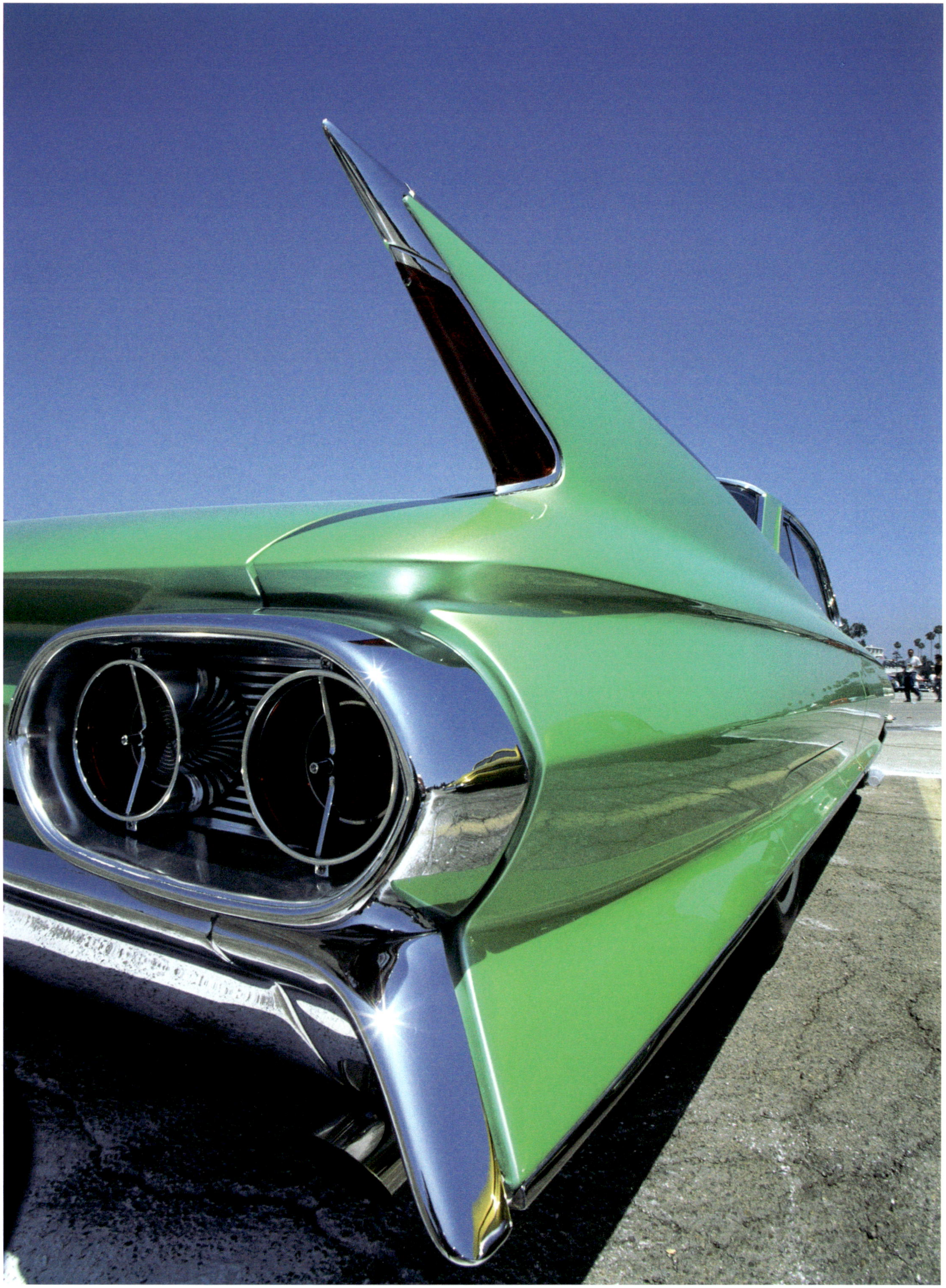

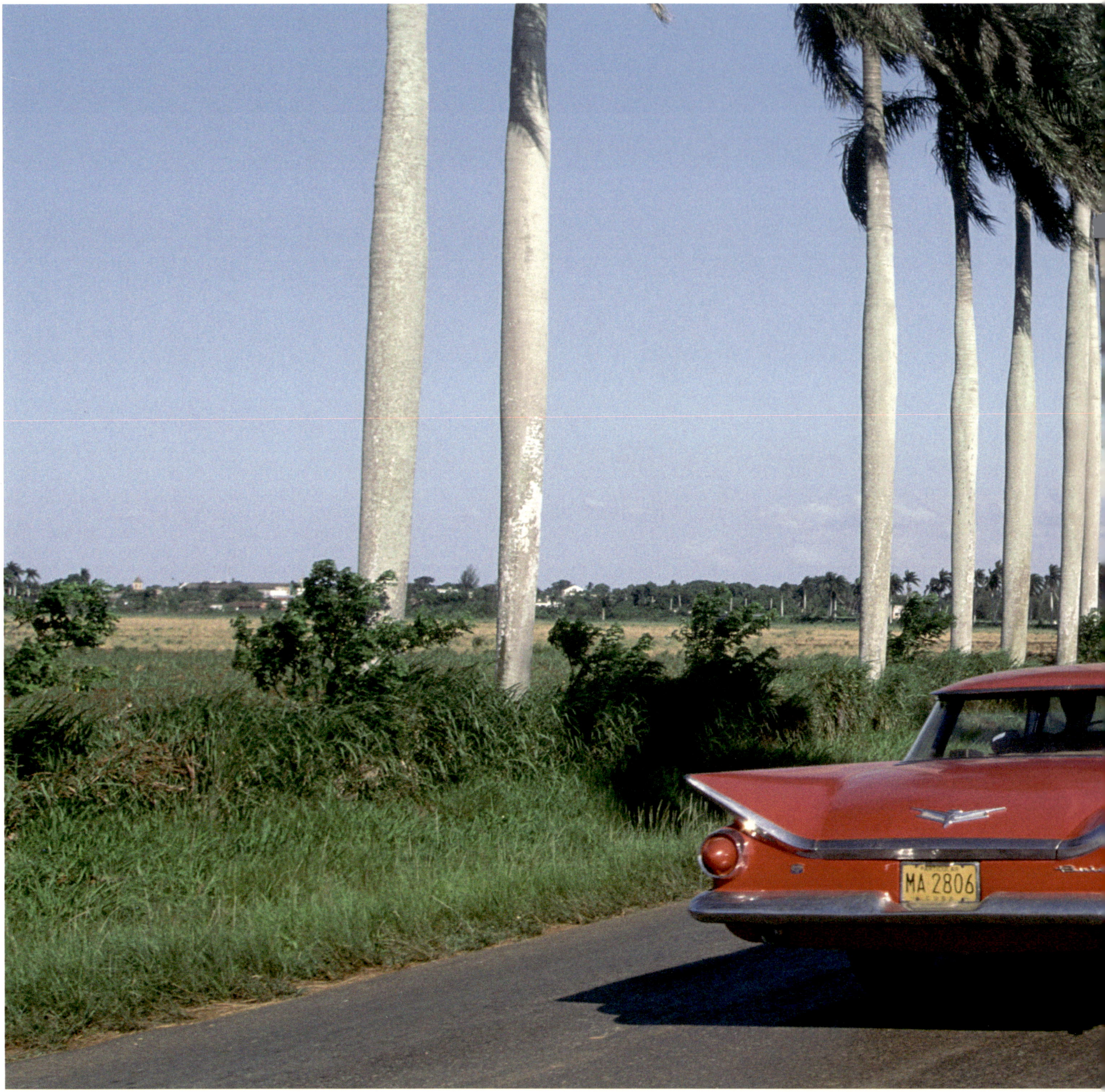
MA 2806

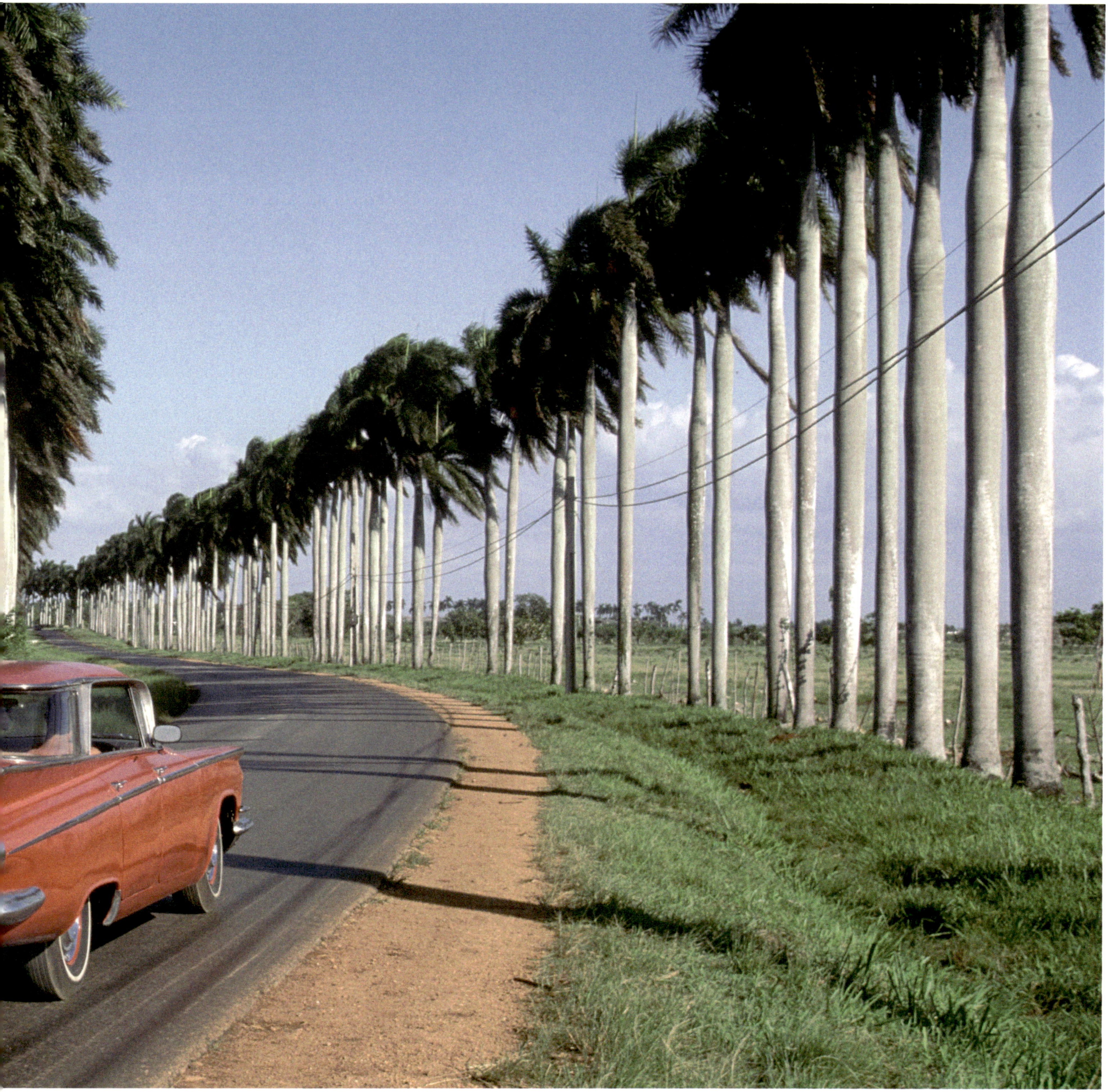

1960 Buick Le Sabre (previous page)
The shiny chrome insignia of a proud past

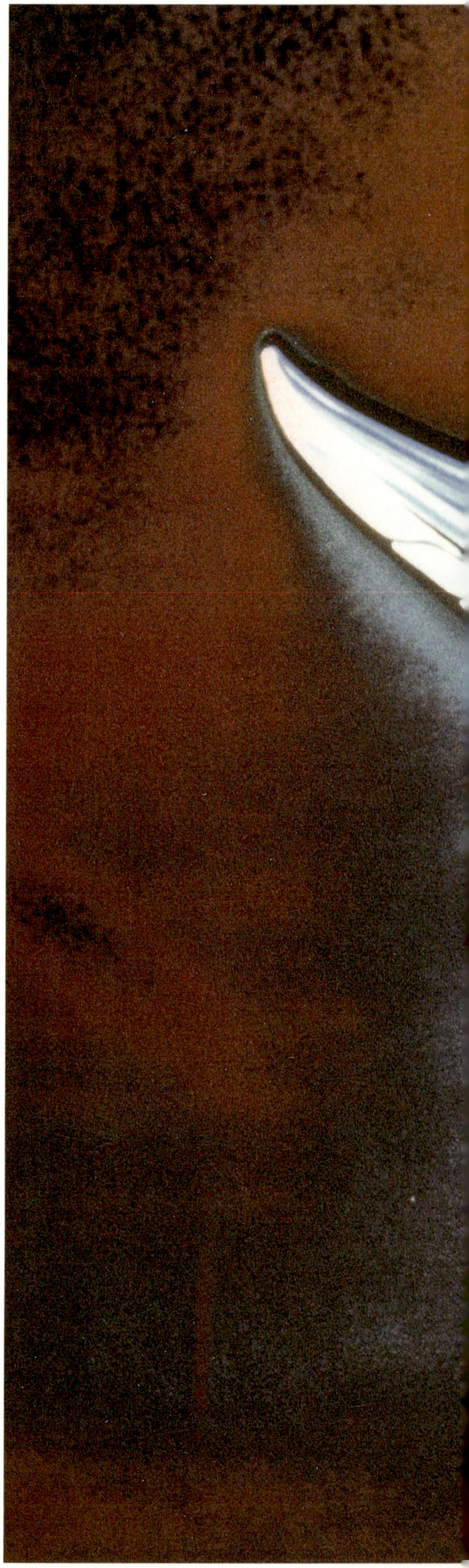

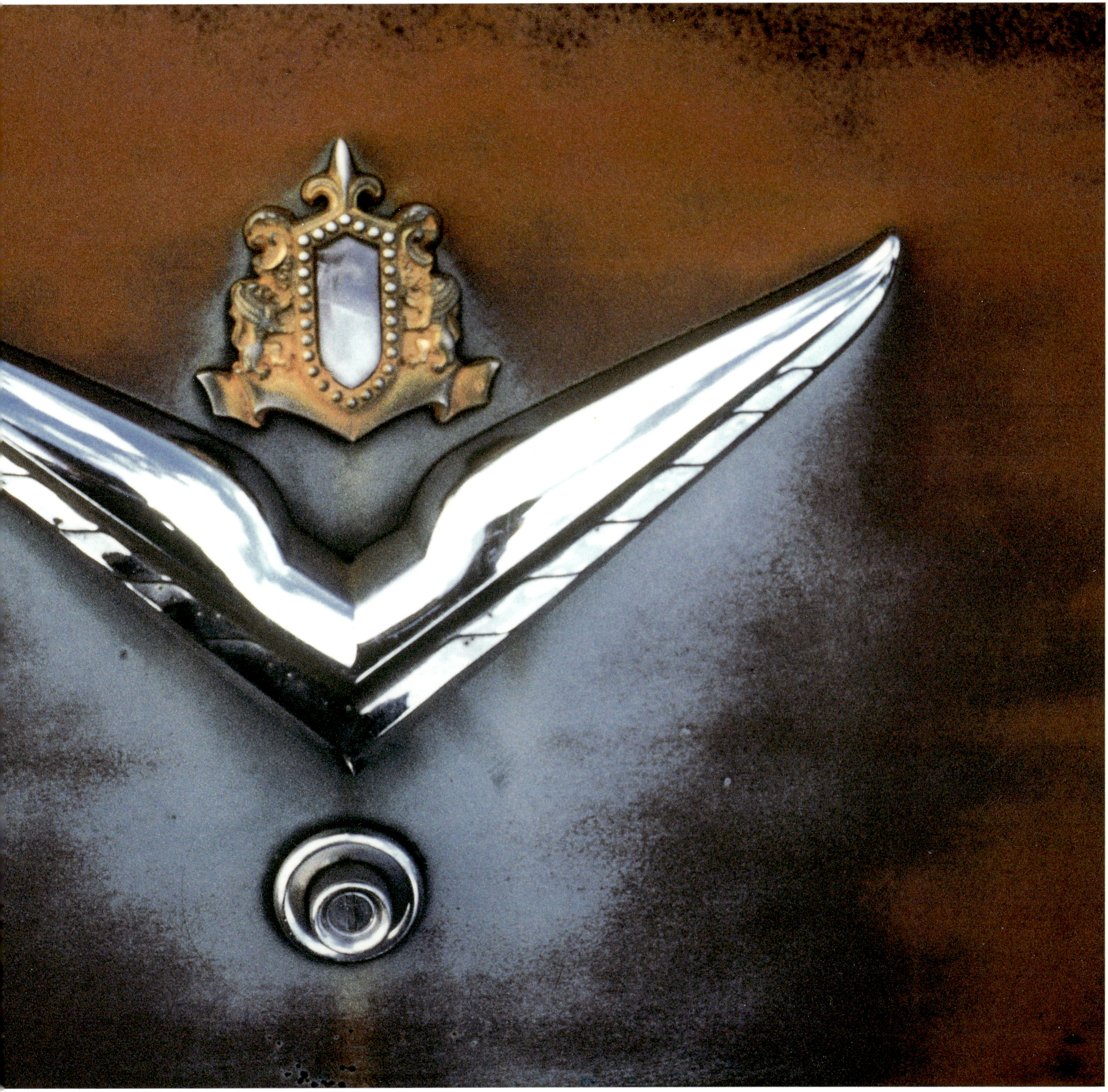

1956 Dodge Royal

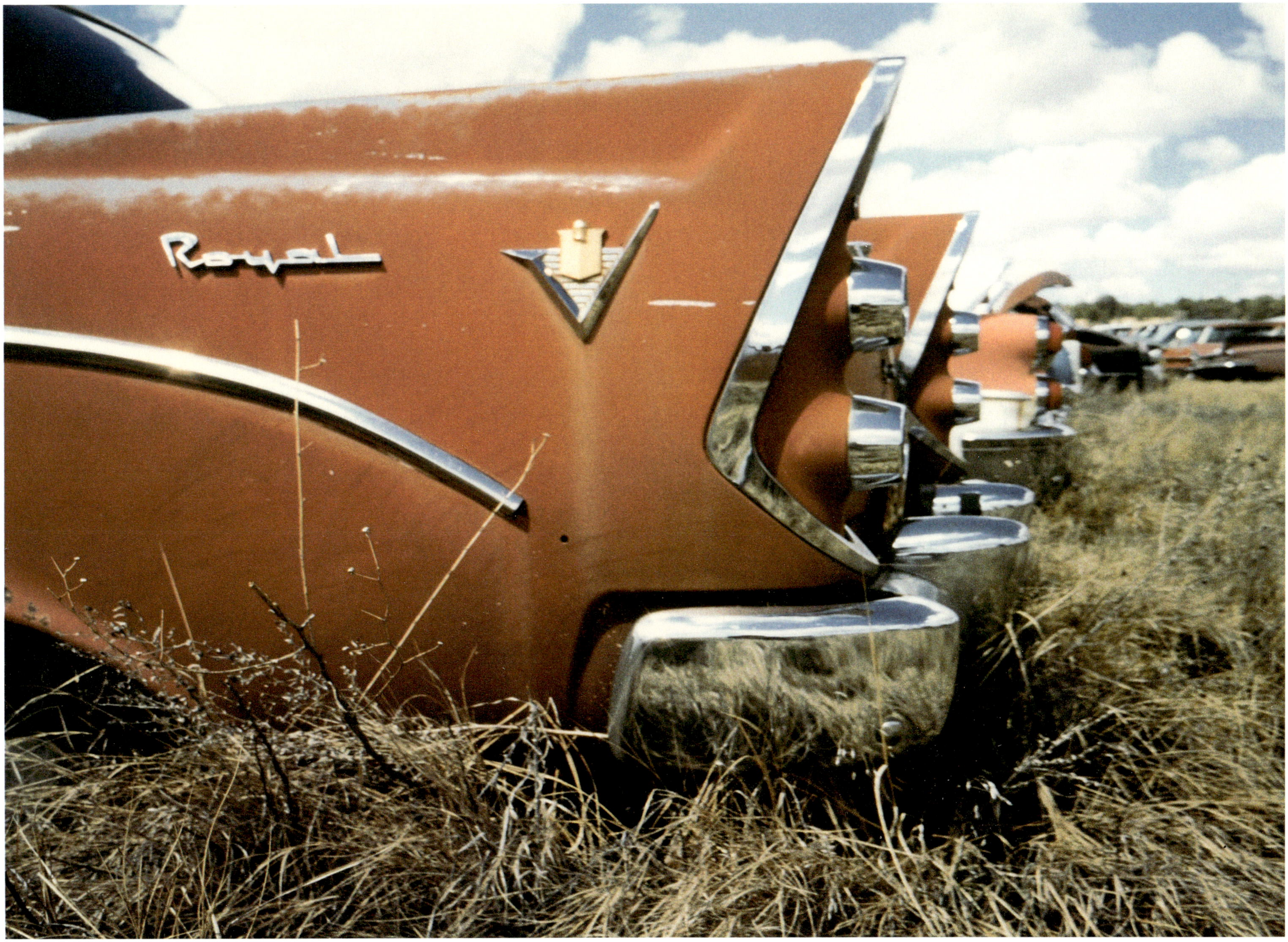
Royal

1950 Buick Roadmaster

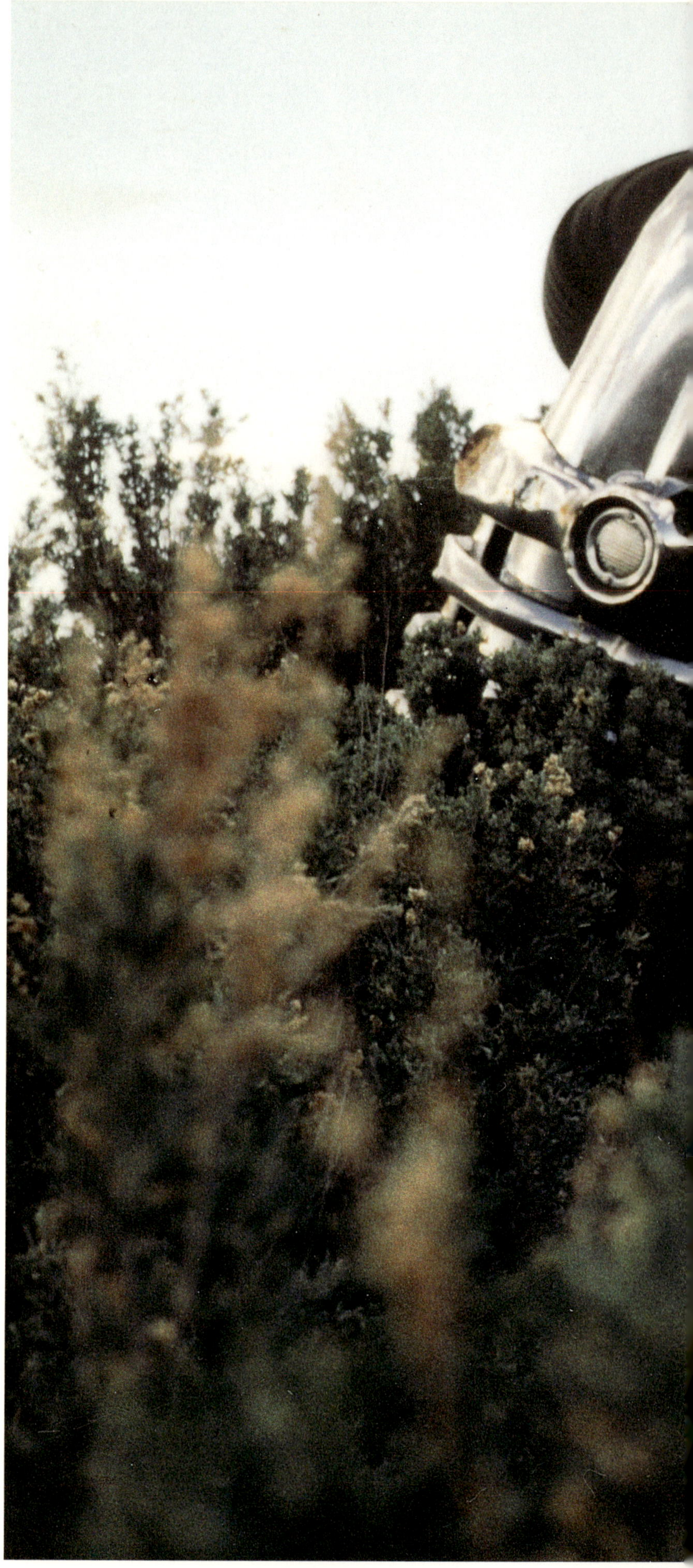

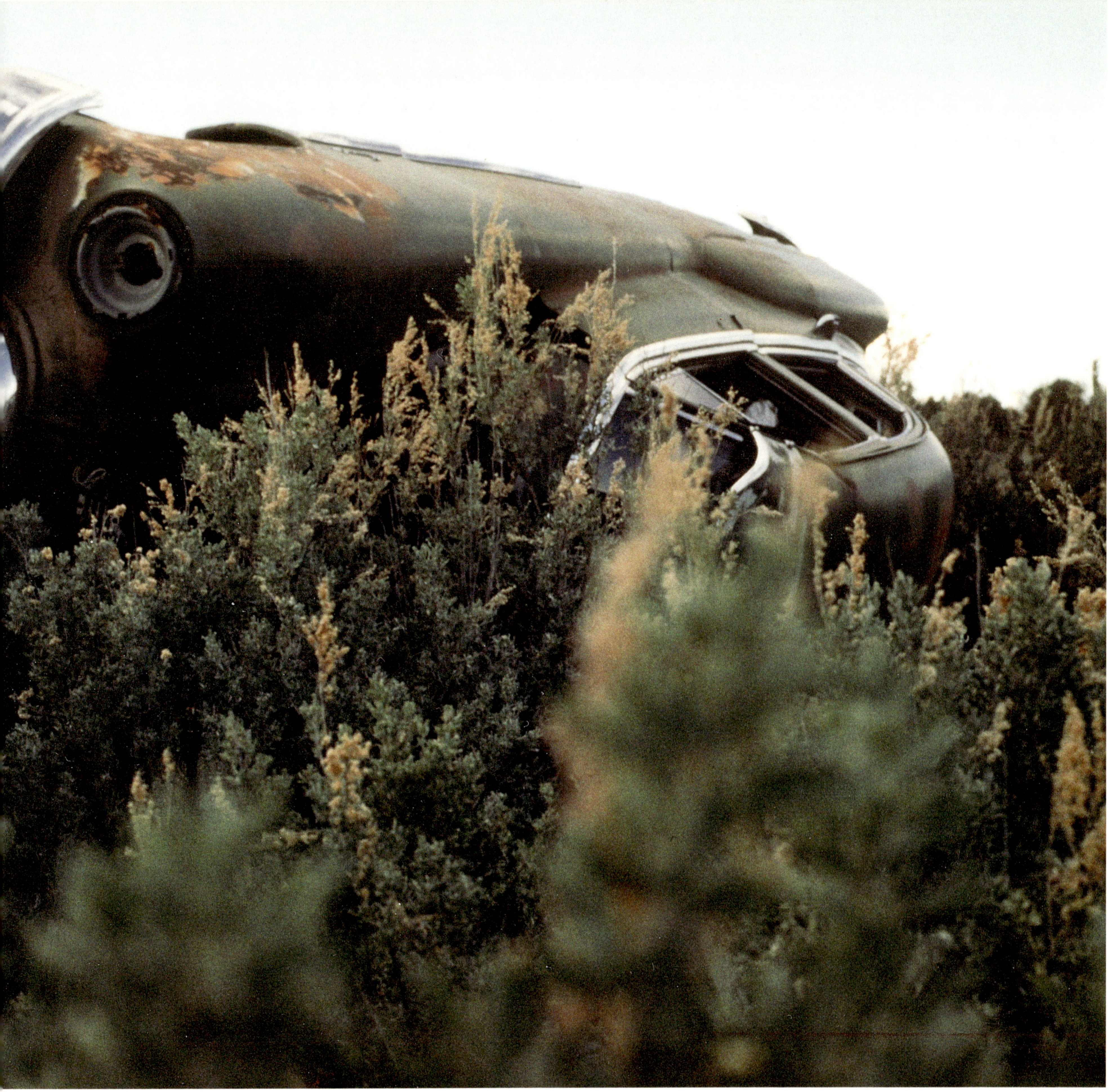

1953 Lincoln Cosmopolitan

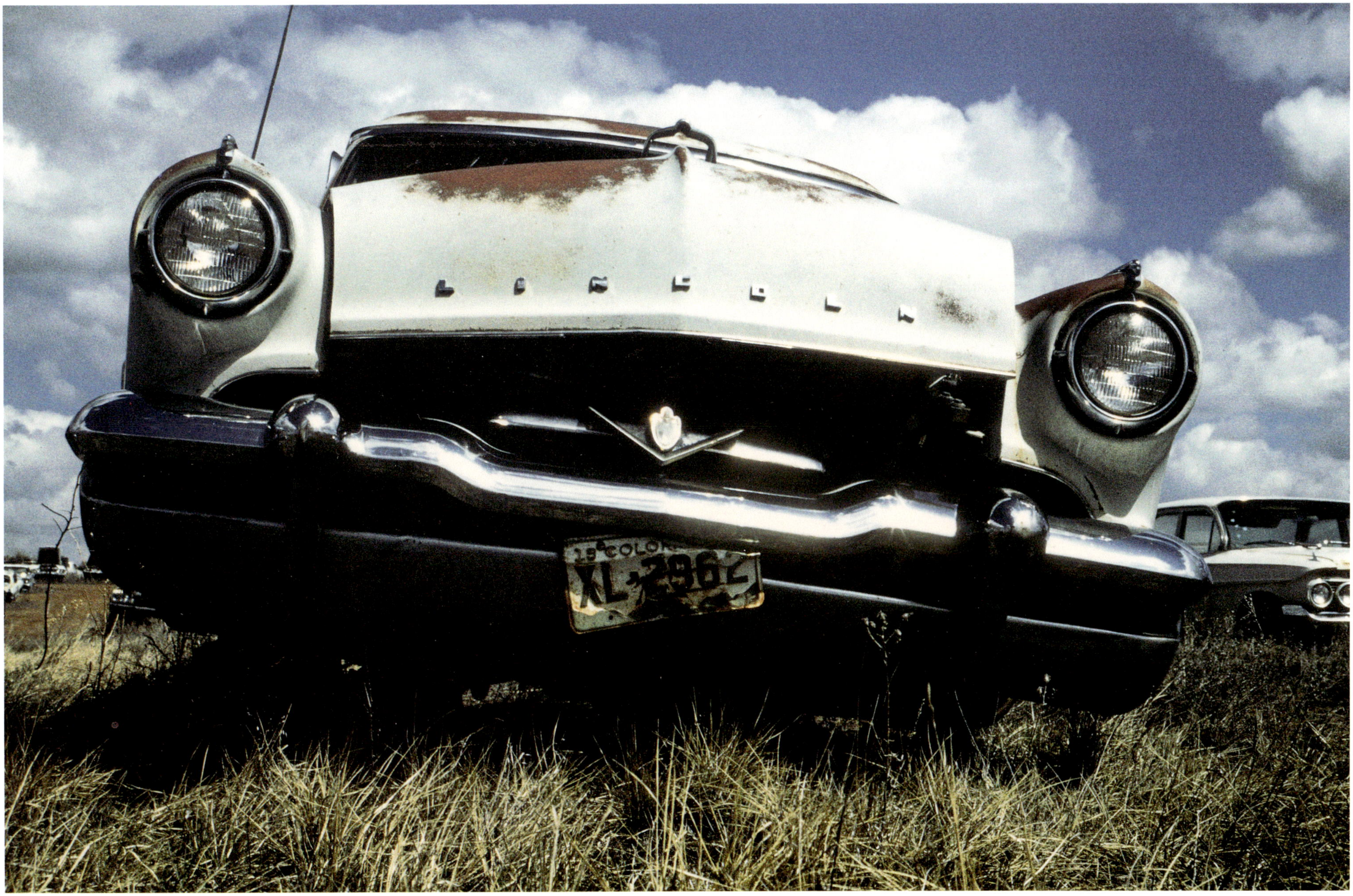
LINCOLN
XL 2962

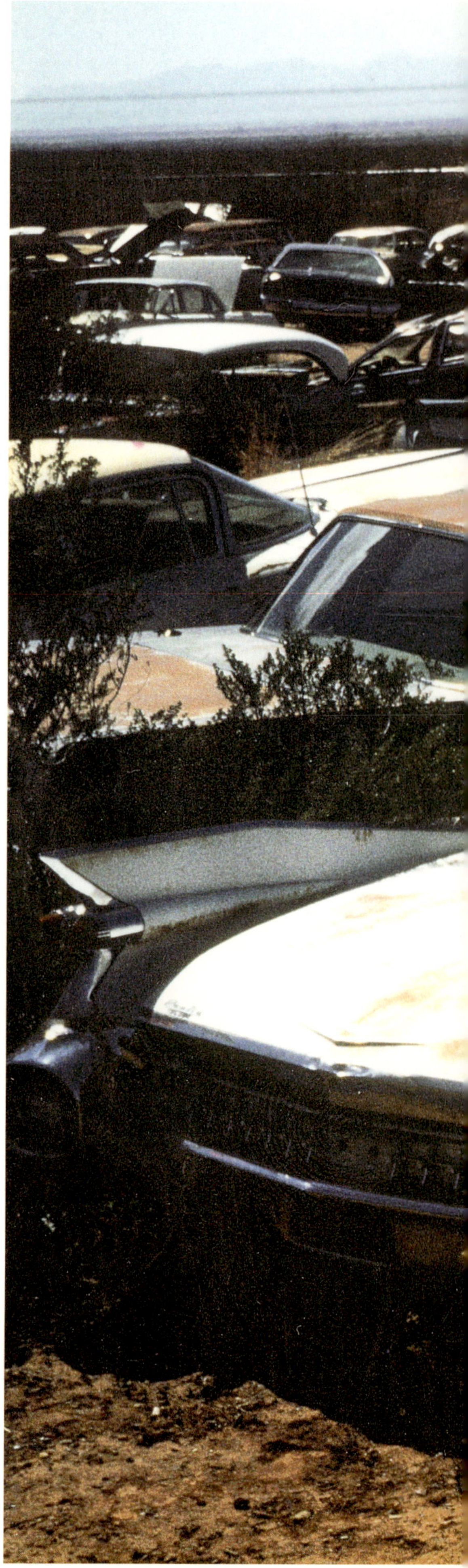

1959 Cadillac Sevilla

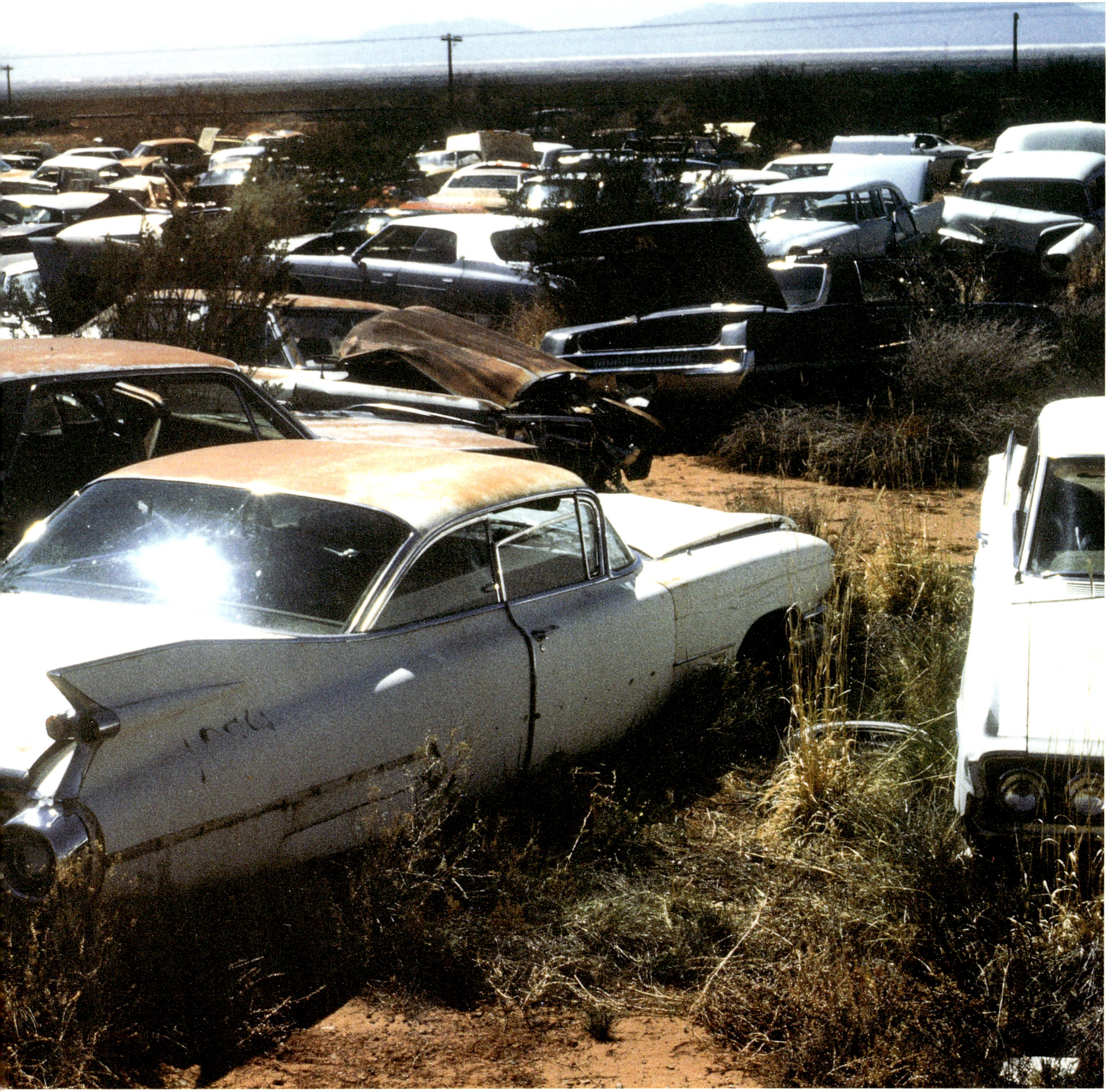

1959 Cadillac Eldorado Convertible

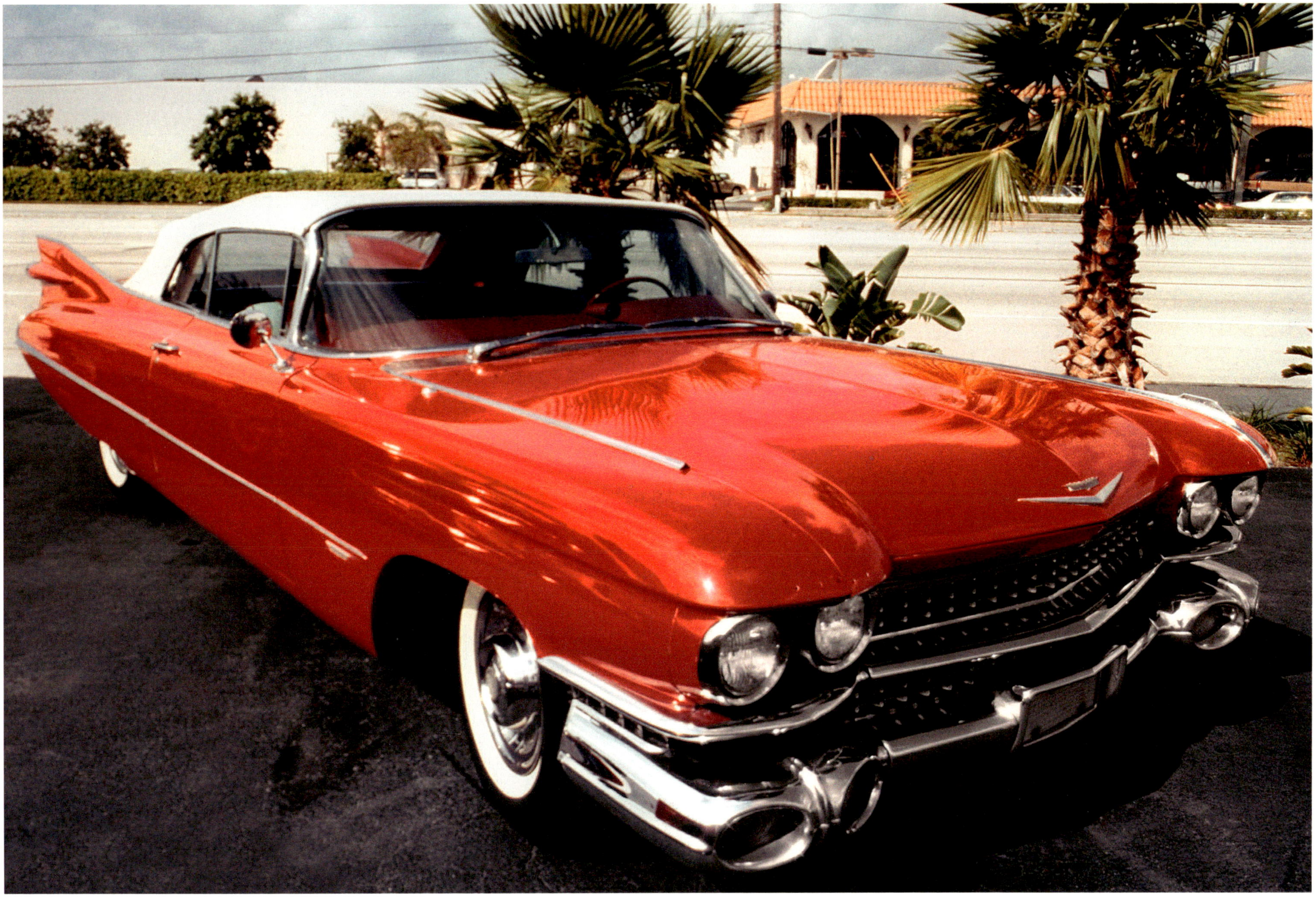

1959 Cadillac Eldorado Convertible

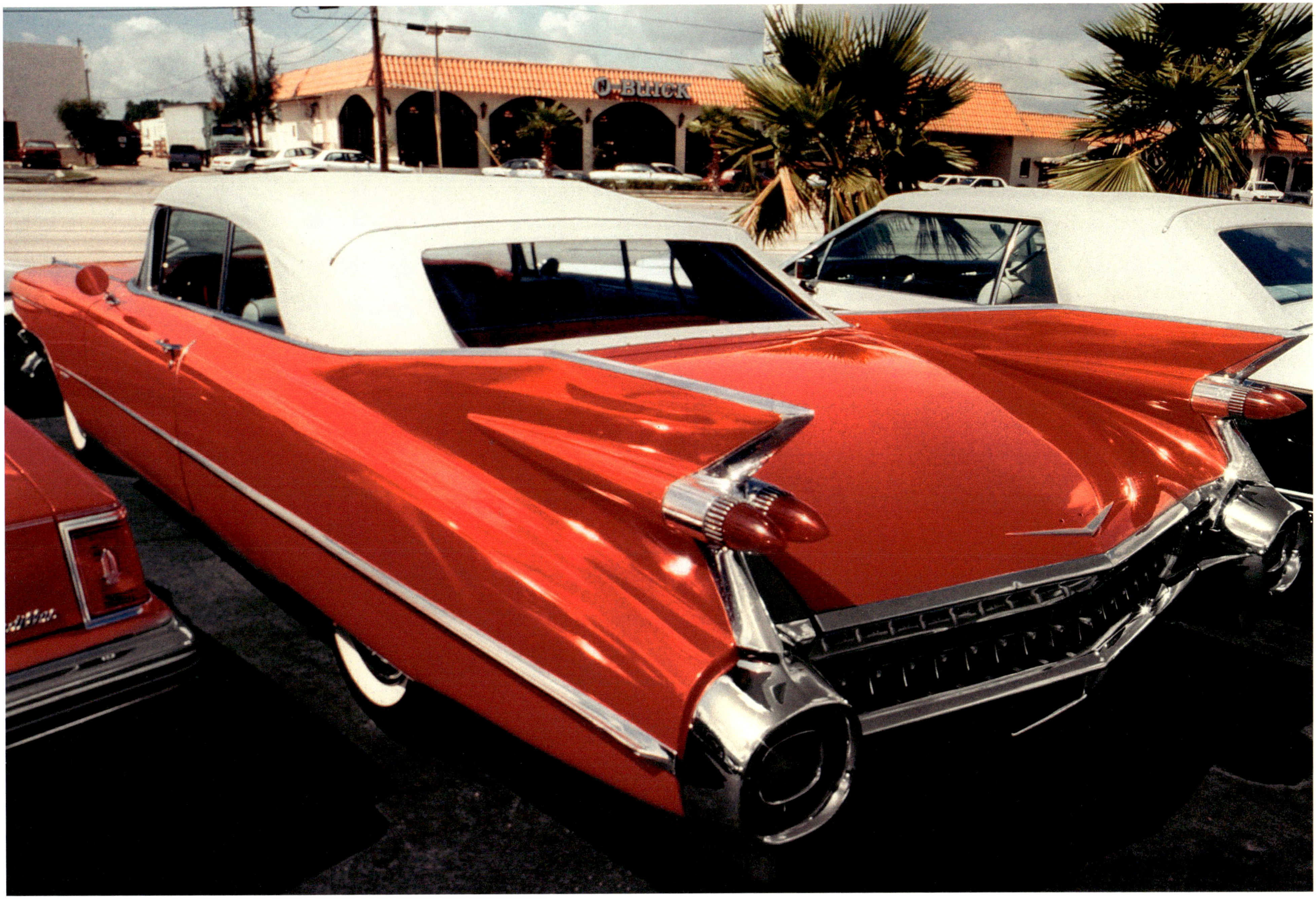
BUICK

AUTOMOBILE CULTURE – A PARKING LOT WITH A SHOWER AND CABLE TV.

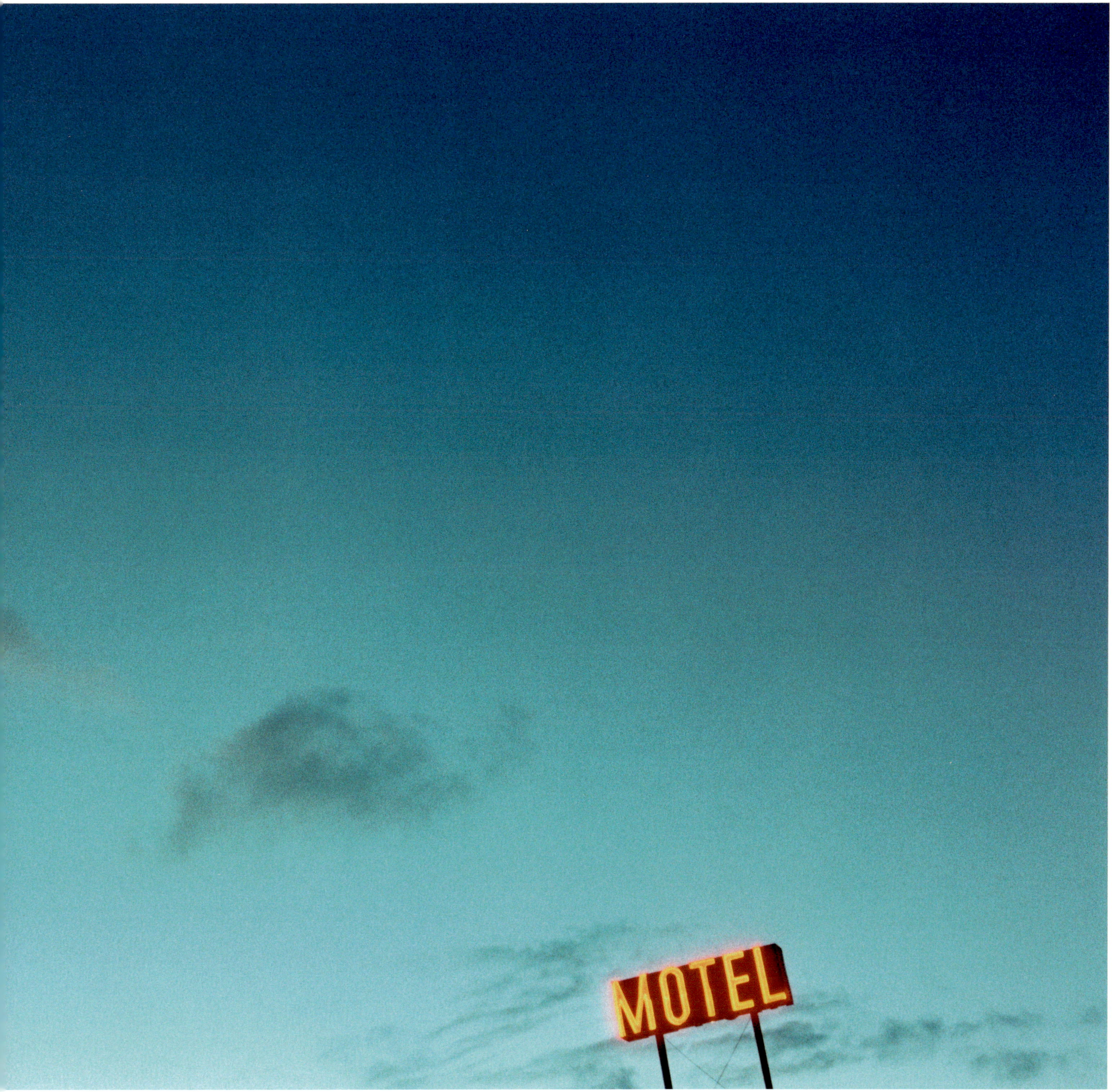
MOTEL

1955 Pontiac Starchief

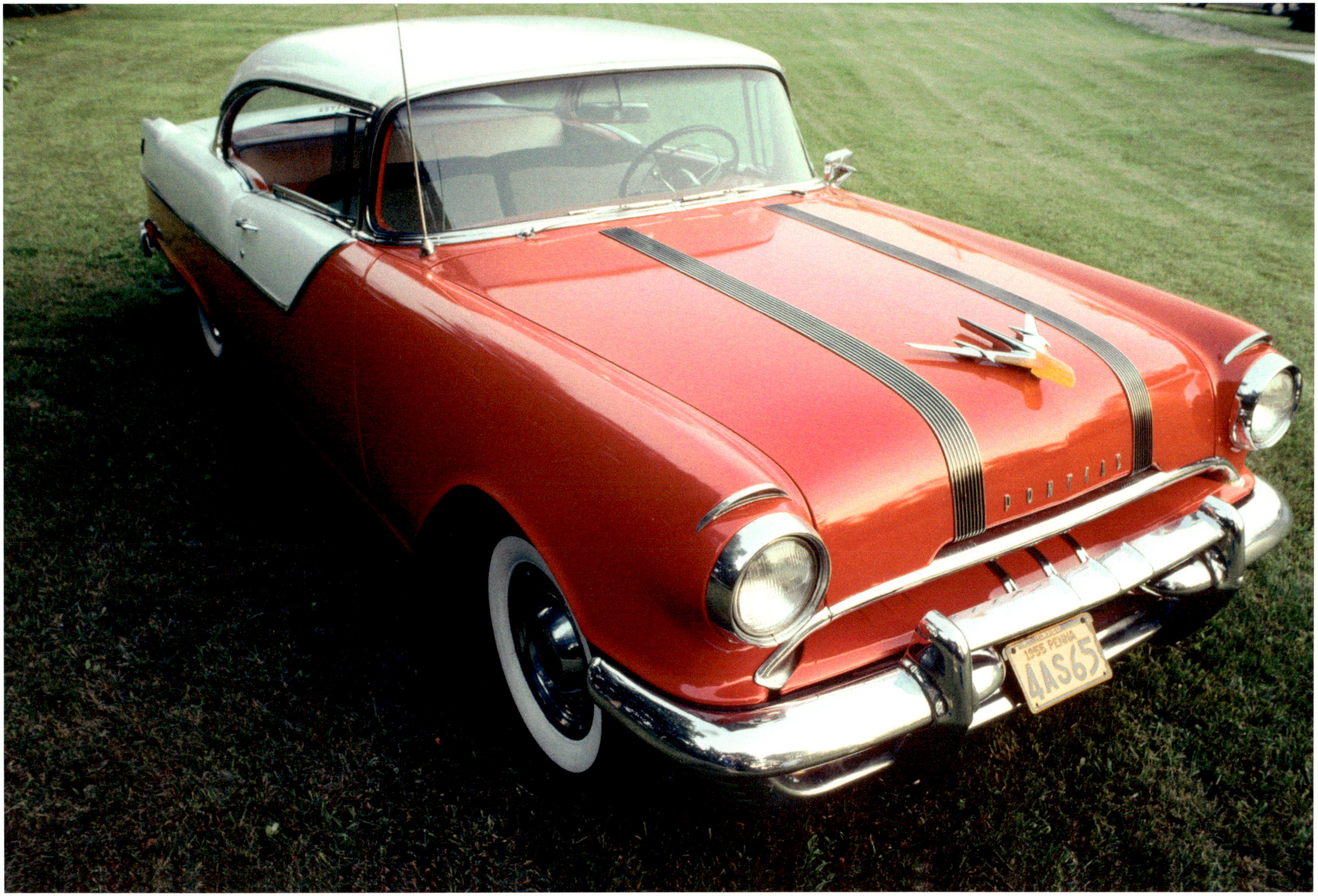
PONTIAC
1955 PENNA
4AS65

TELL ME WHAT CAR YOU DRIVE
AND I WILL TELL YOU WHO YOU WANT TO BE.

1957 Chevrolet Bel Air

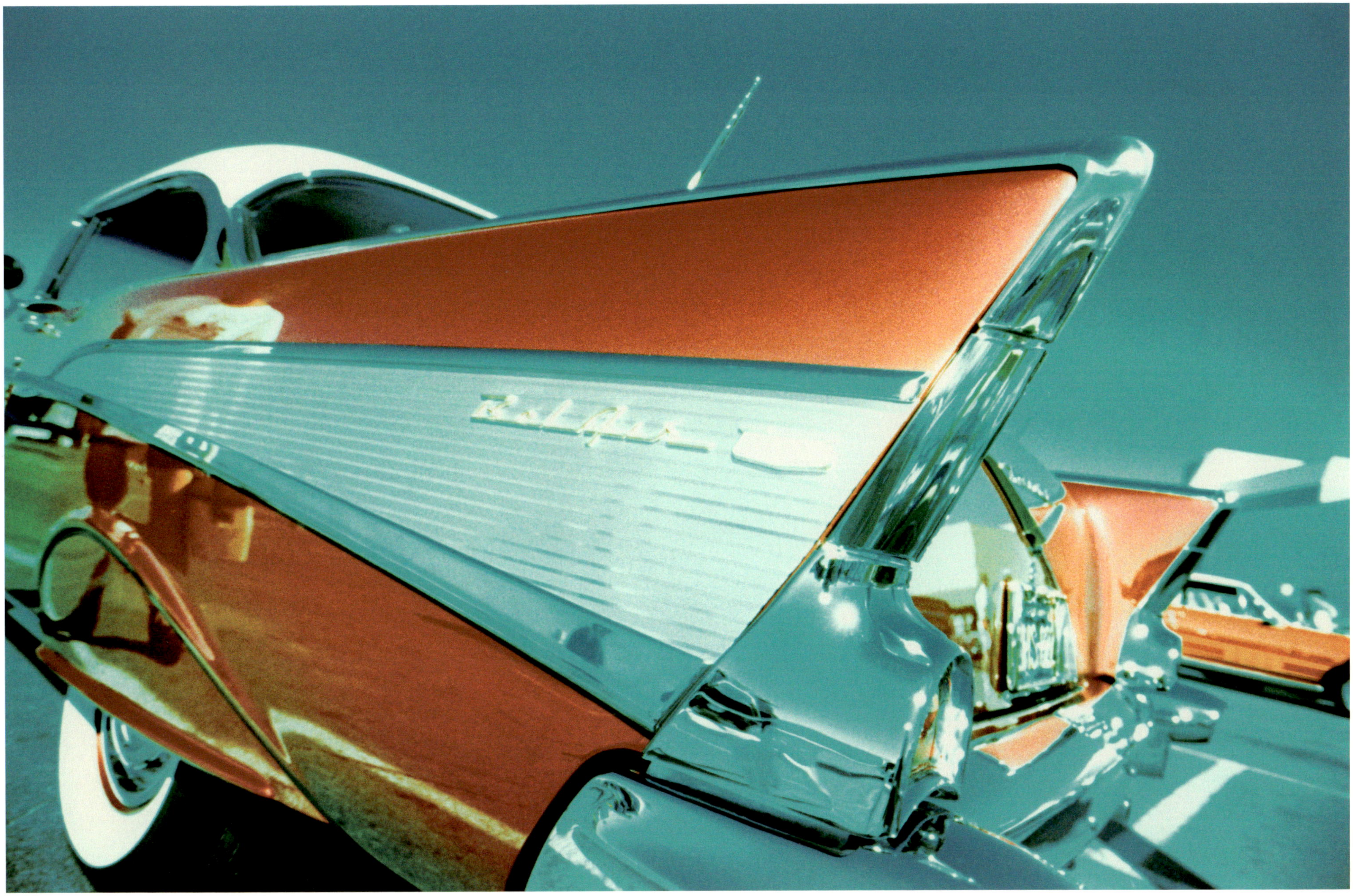

1966 Cadillac De Ville

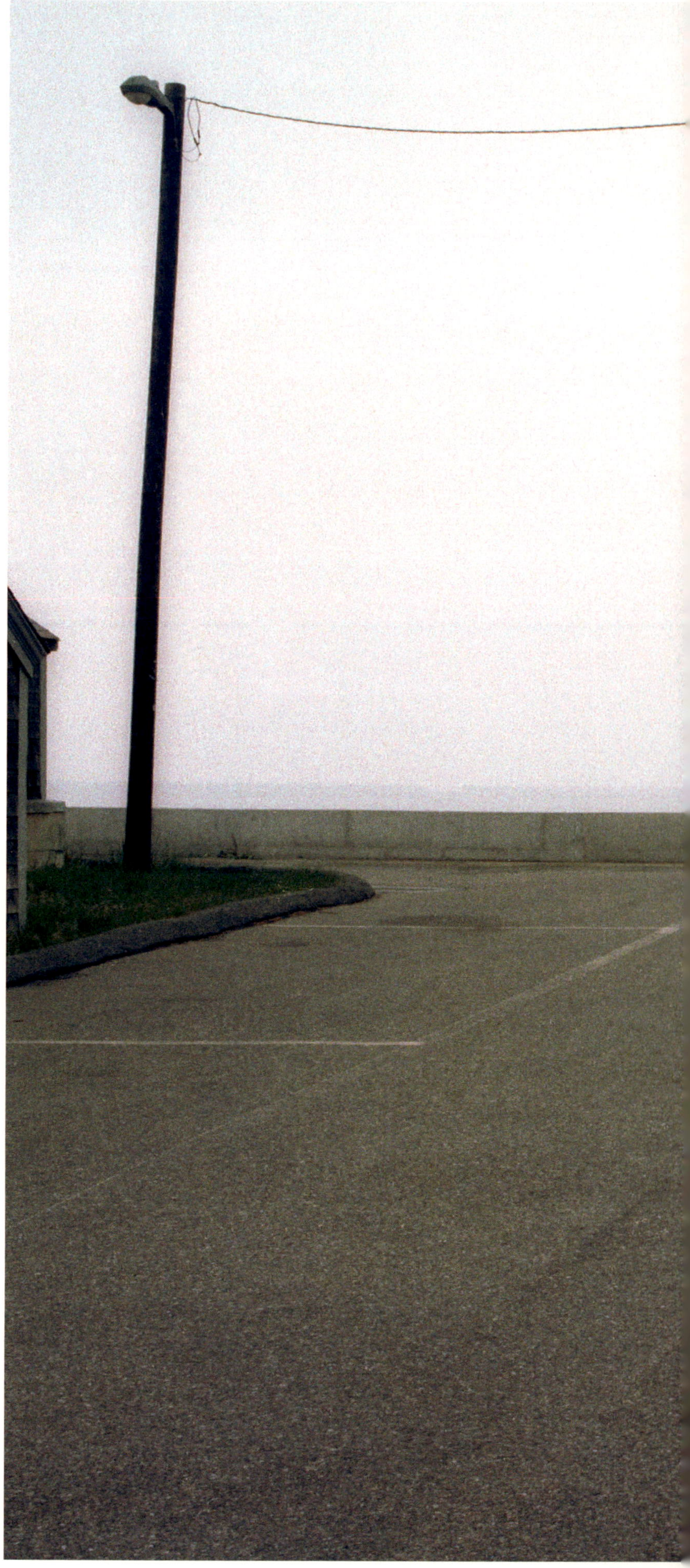

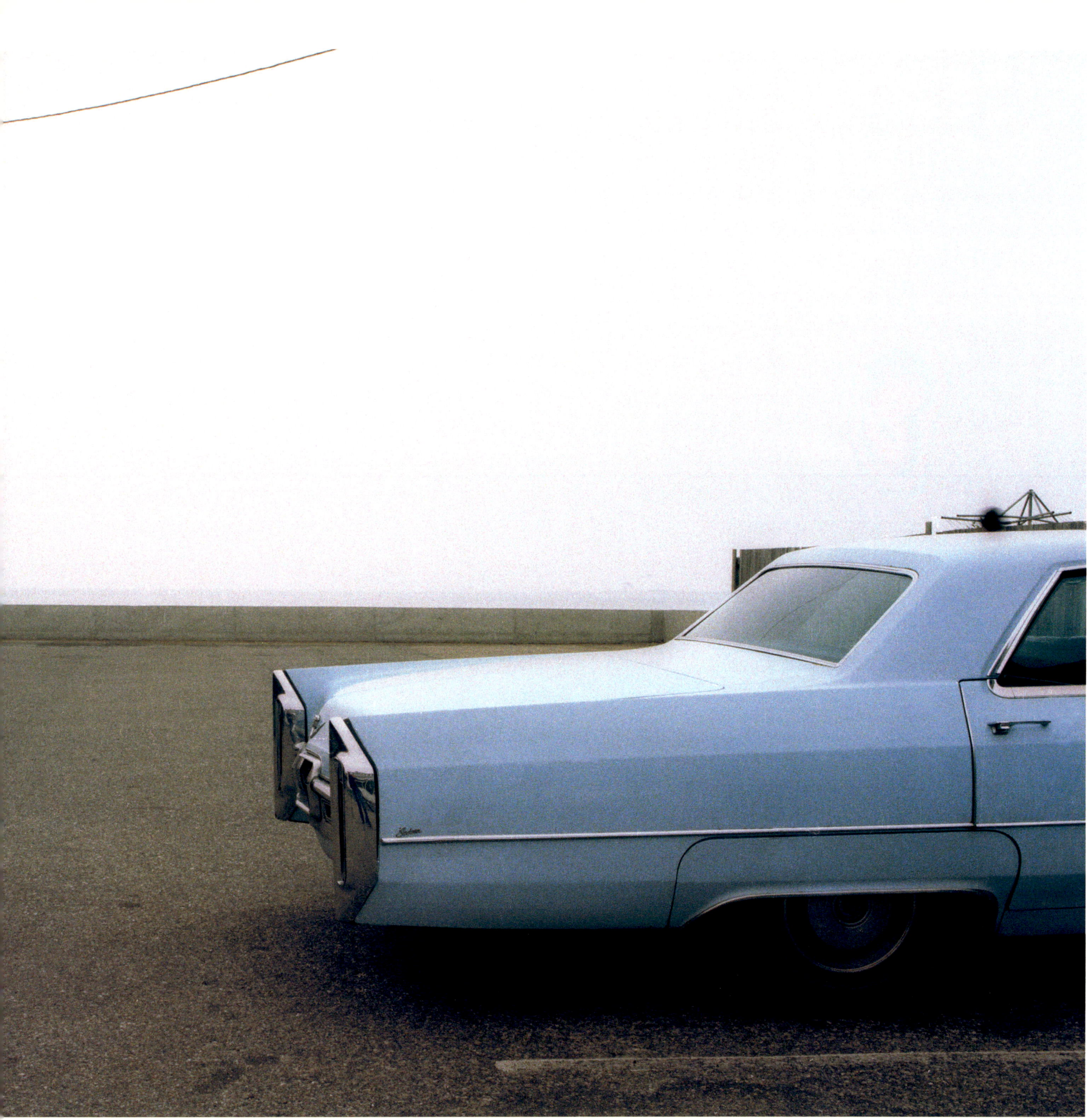

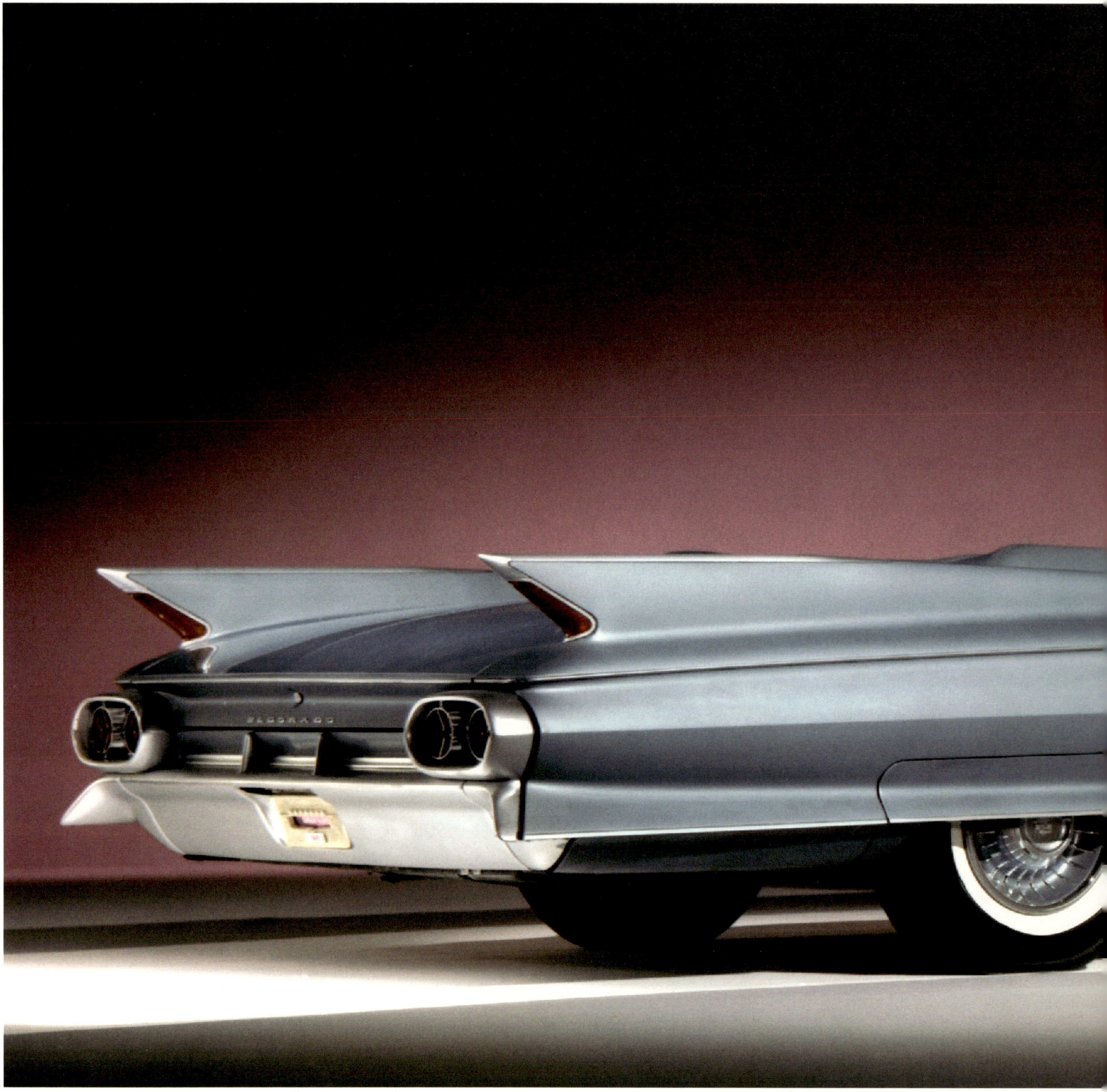

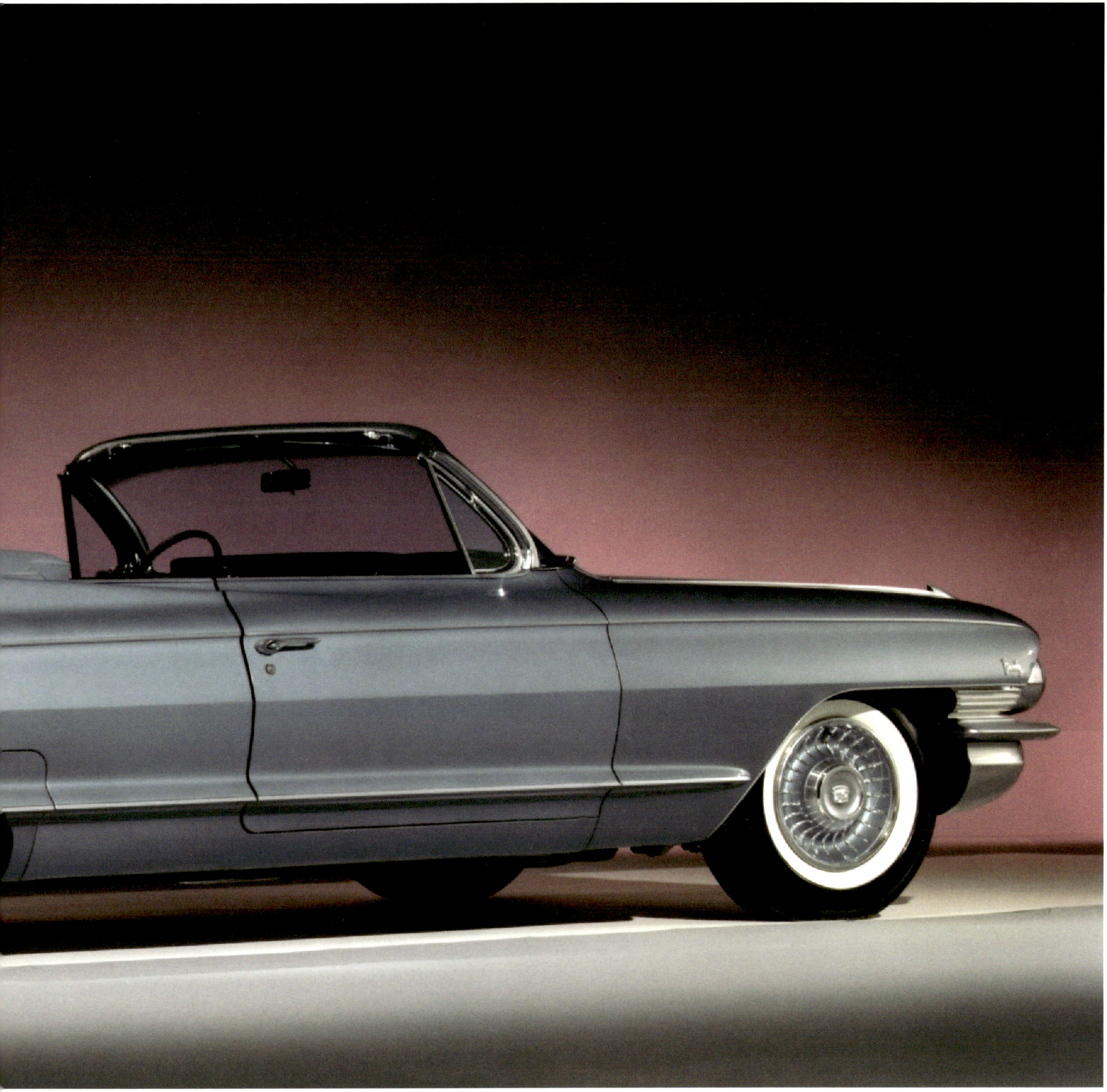

KITSCH AND GLAMOUR – YOU ONLY GET ONE CHANCE TO LEAVE A FIRST IMPRESSION.

1961 Cadillac Eldorado (previous page)
New Cadillacs roll into the paint dryer at their assembly plant (1968 Detroit, Michigan, USA).

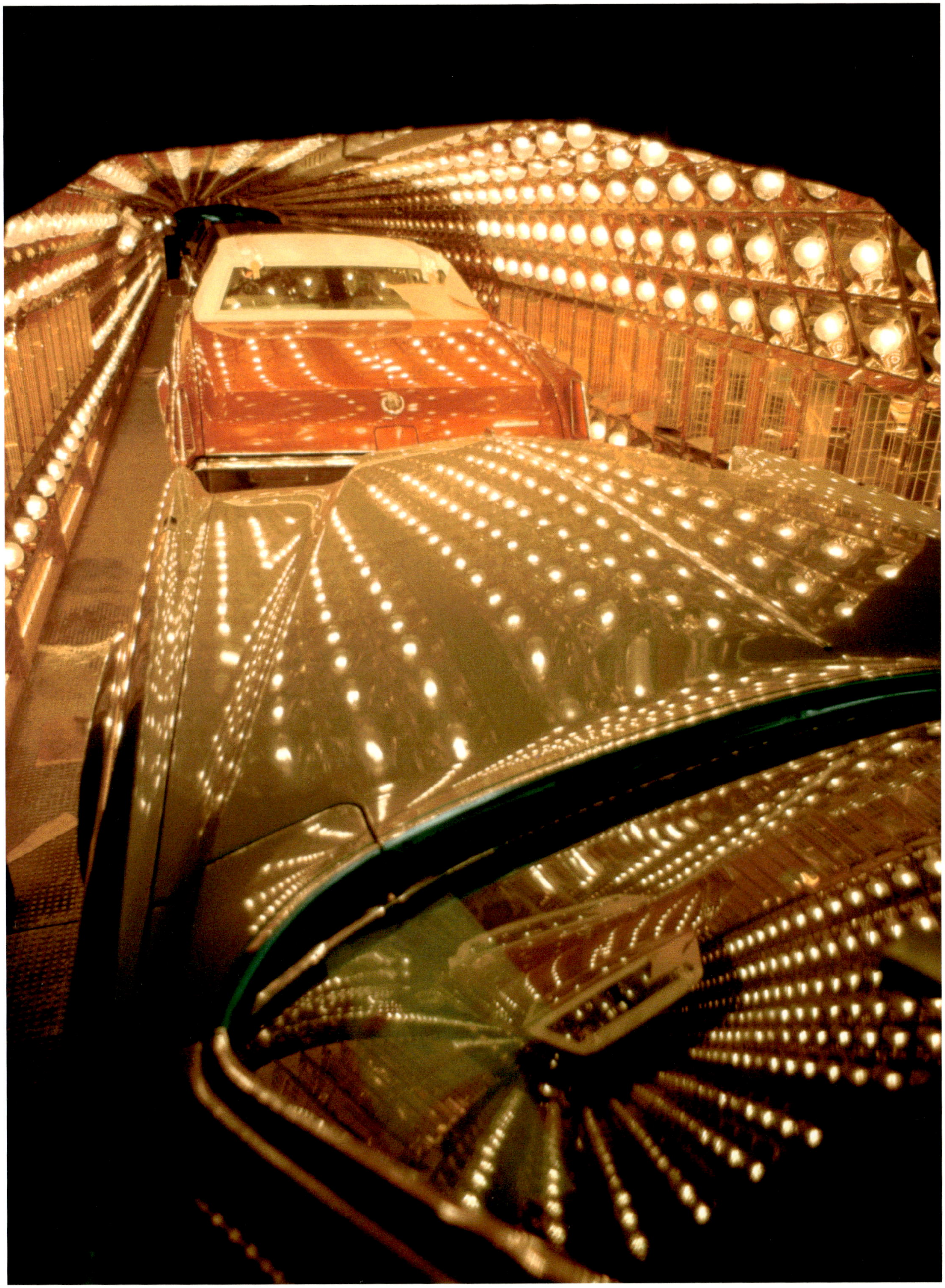

1959 Cadillac Eldorado

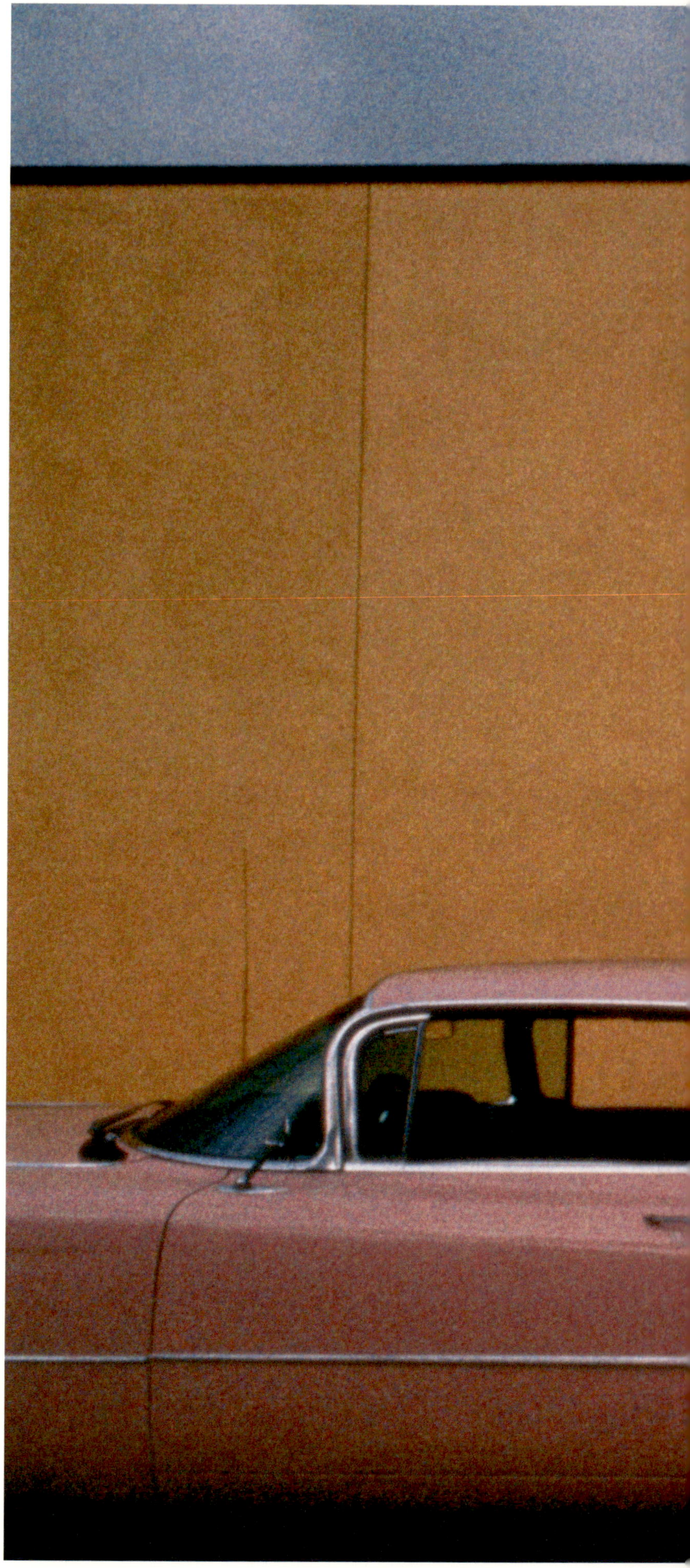

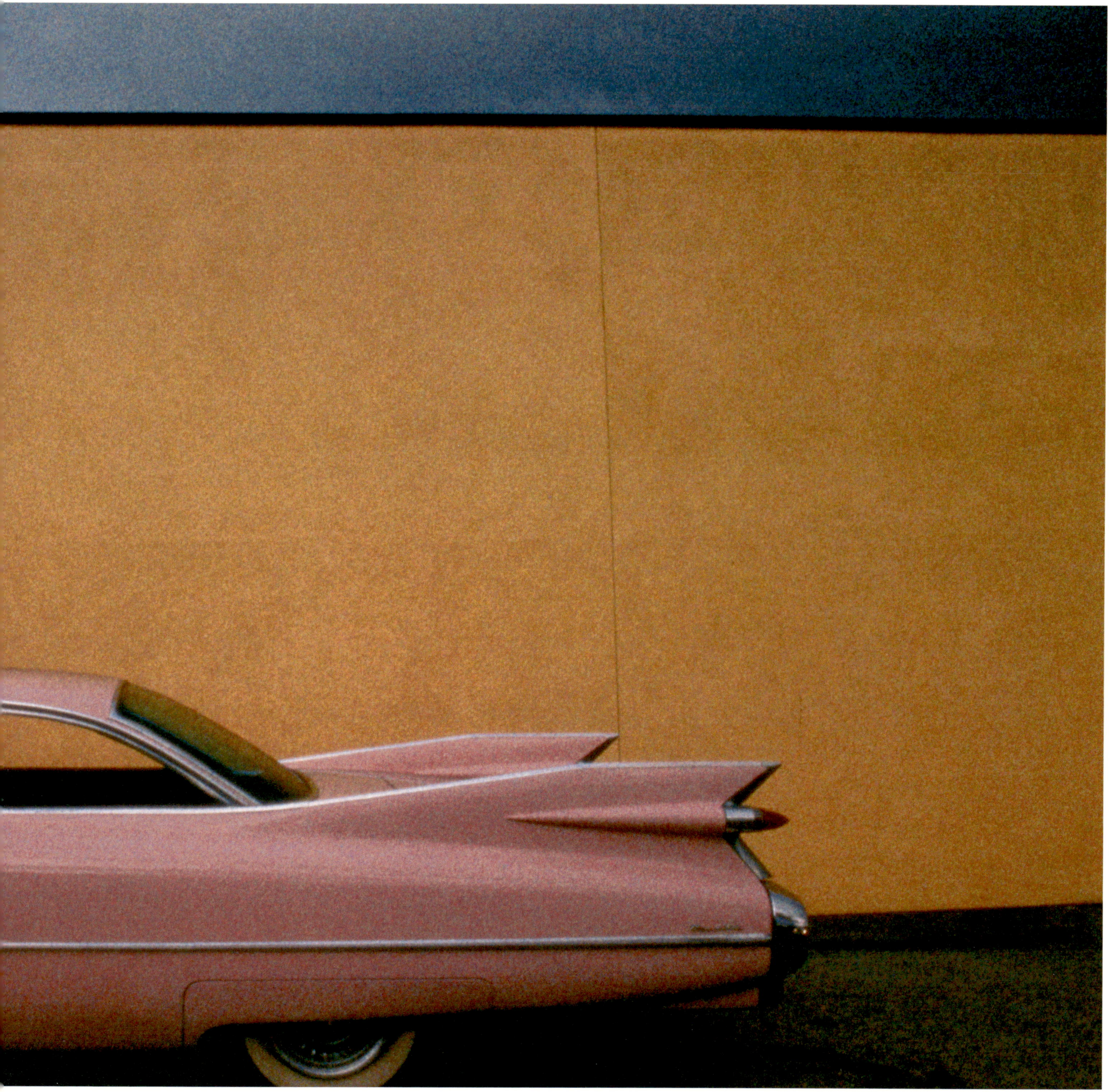

THE ROAD IS A STAGE.
ARE YOU READY FOR A LEAD ROLE?

1957 Chevrolet Bel Air Convertible

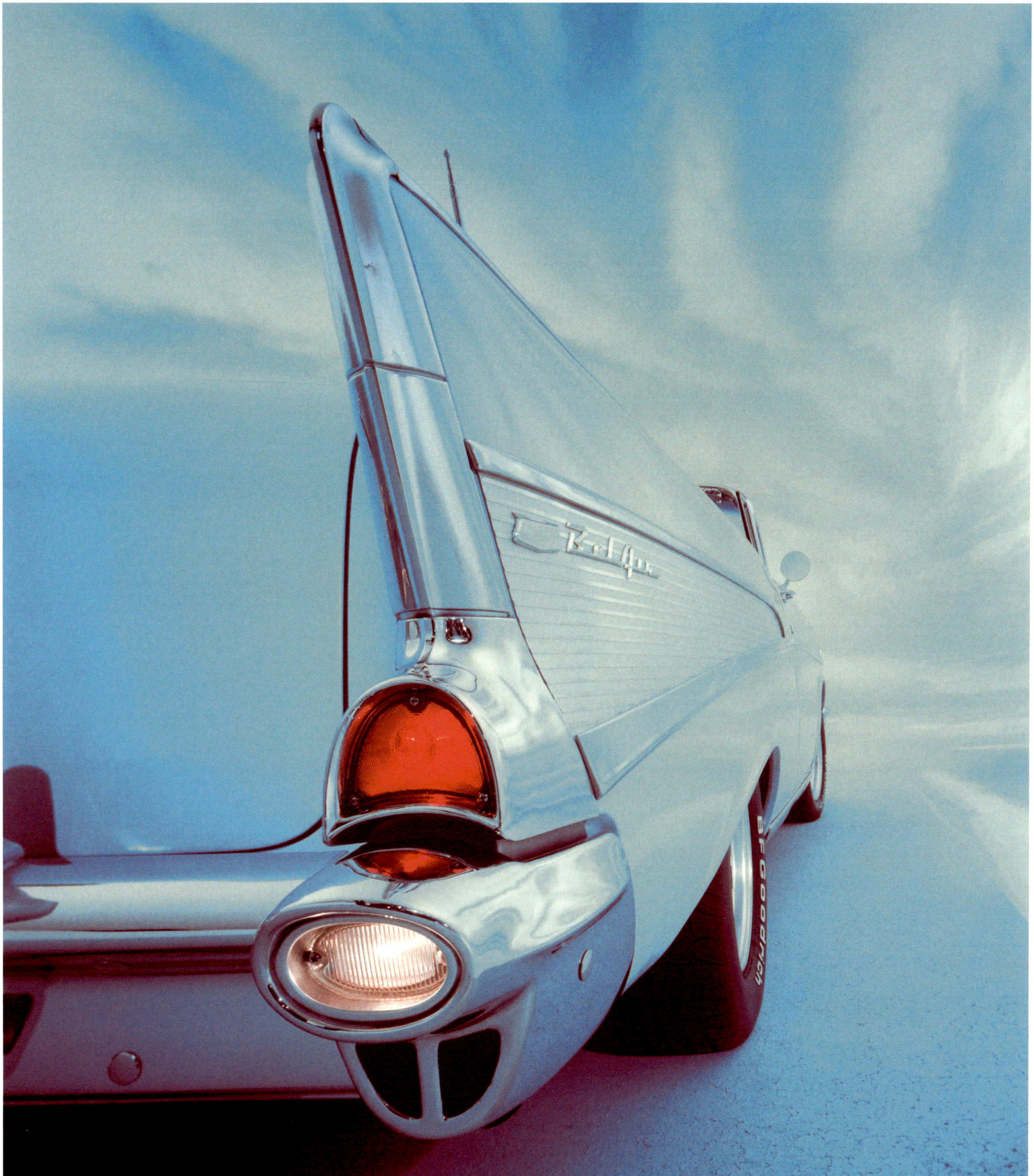
BFGoodrich

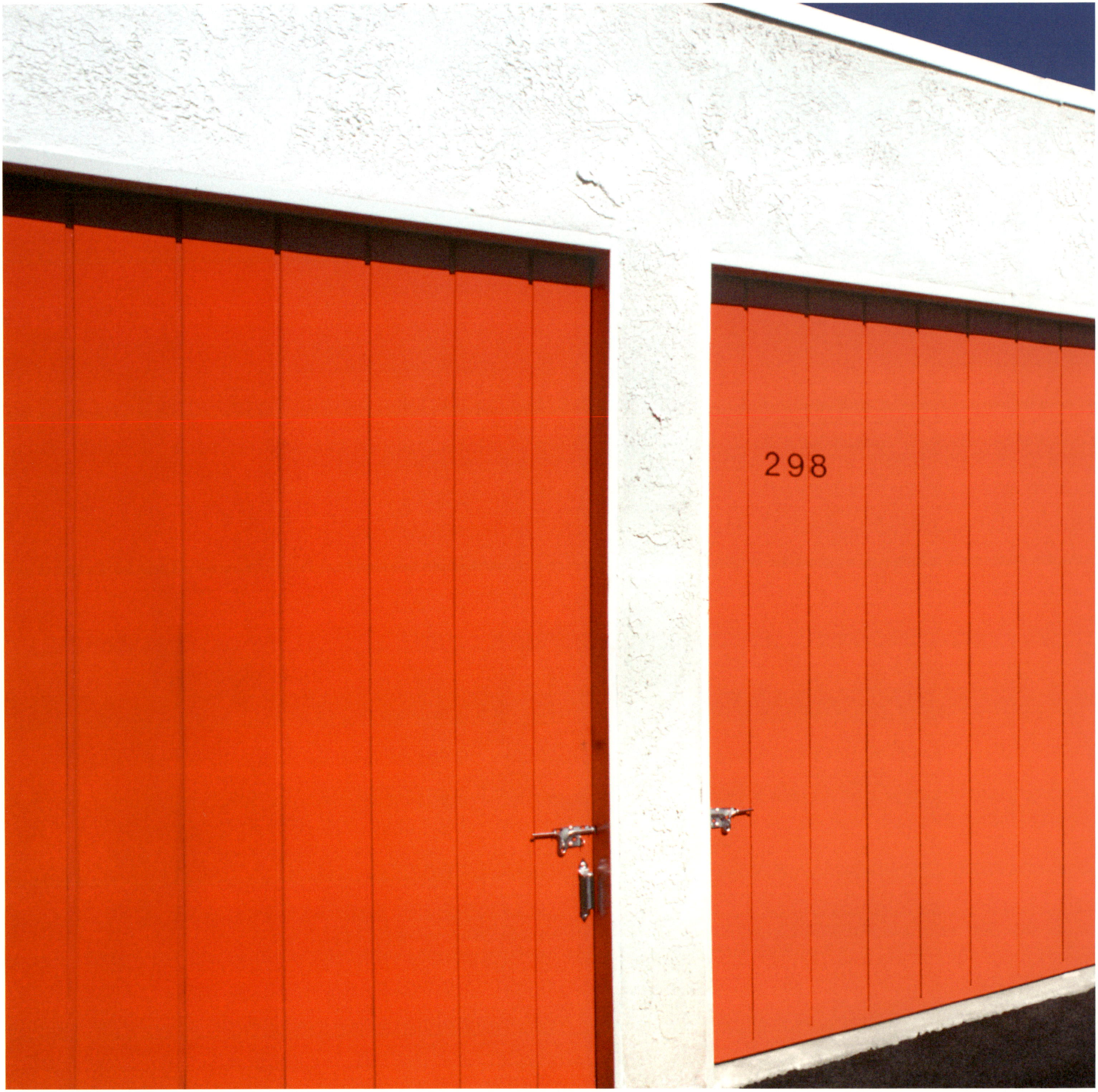
298

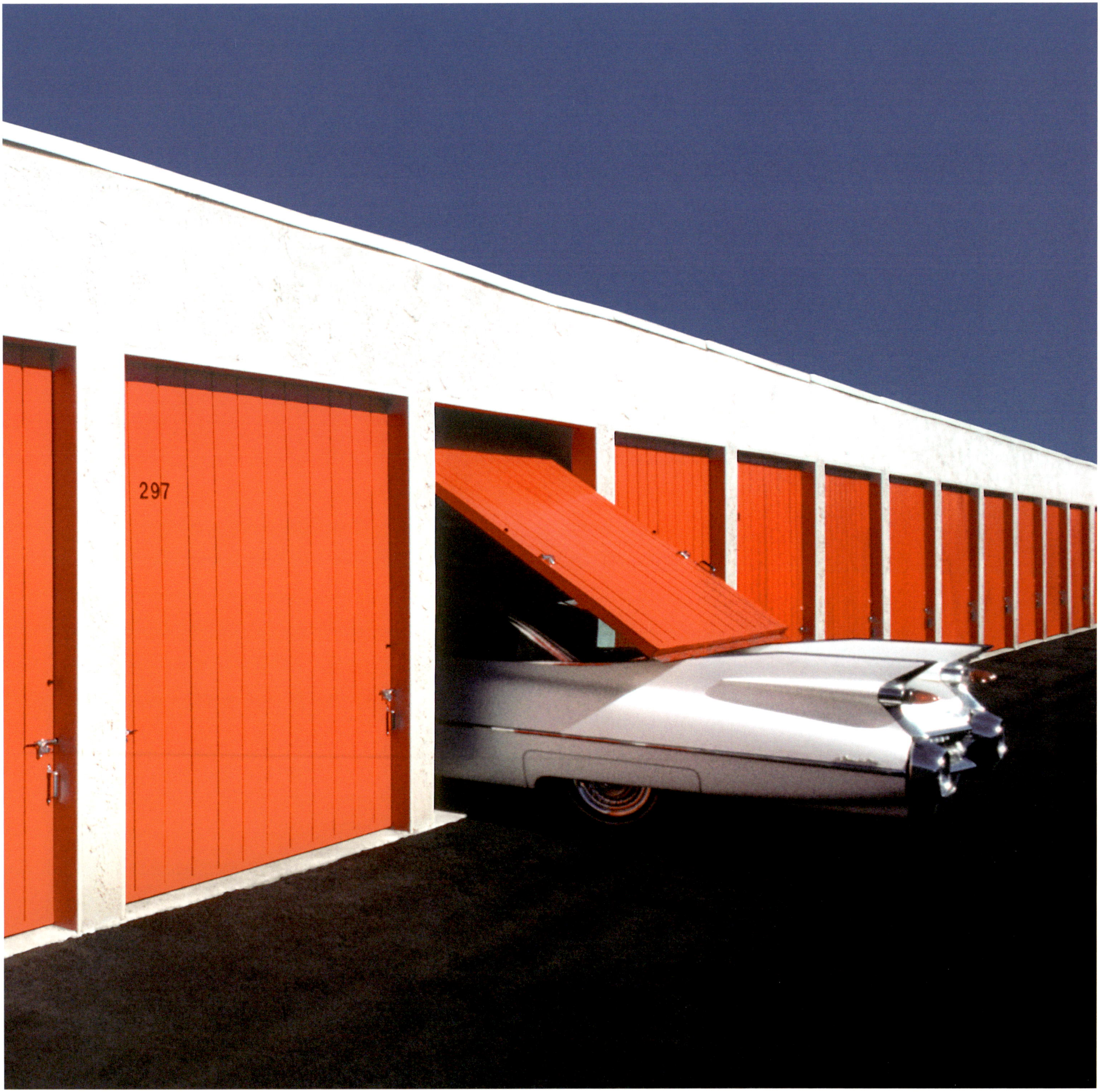
297

FULL STOP – EVERY TIME YOU FILL UP IS AN OPPORTUNITY TO SET NEW GOALS.

1959 Cadillac Eldorado (previous page)
1986 Pontiac Grand Prix

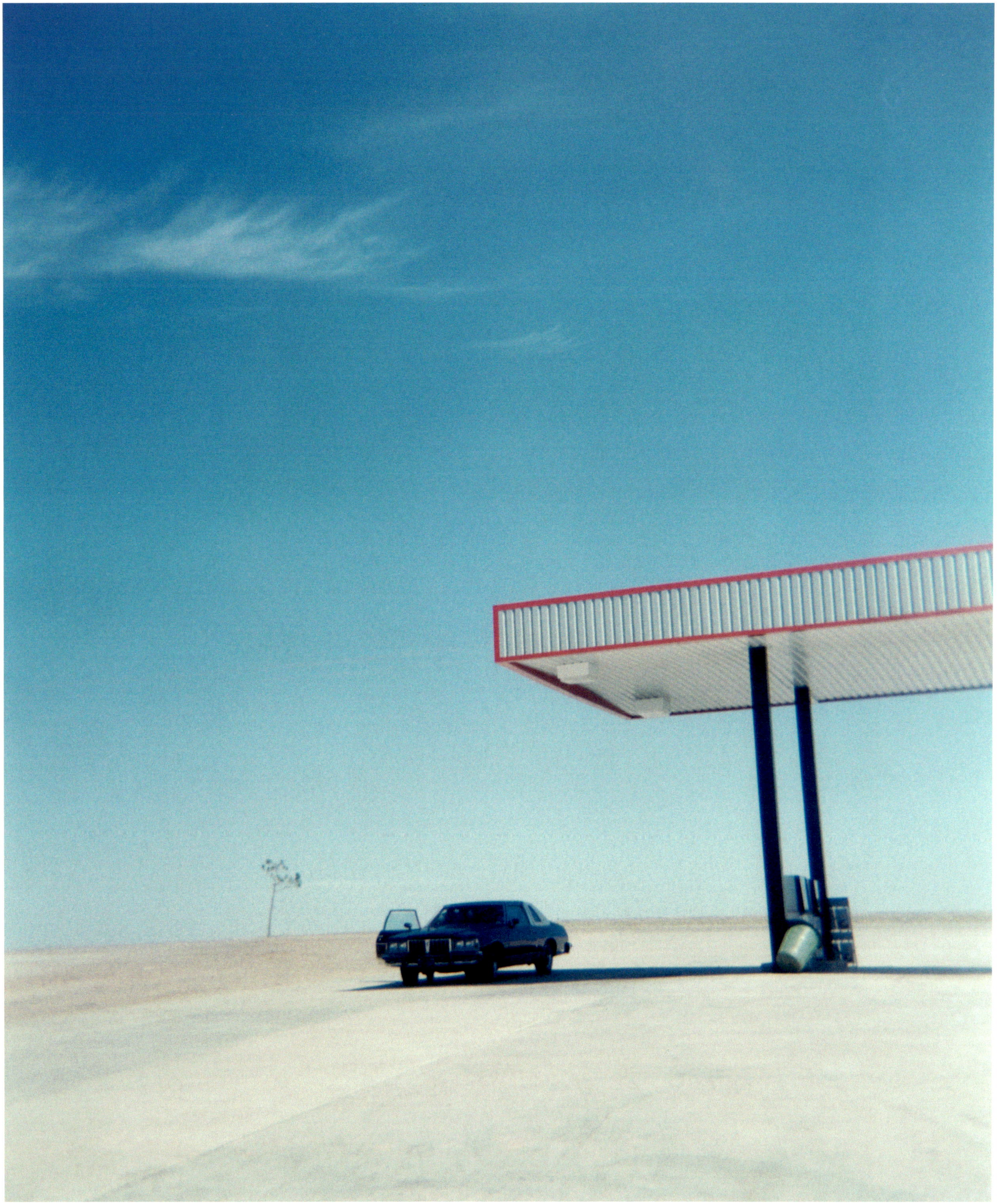

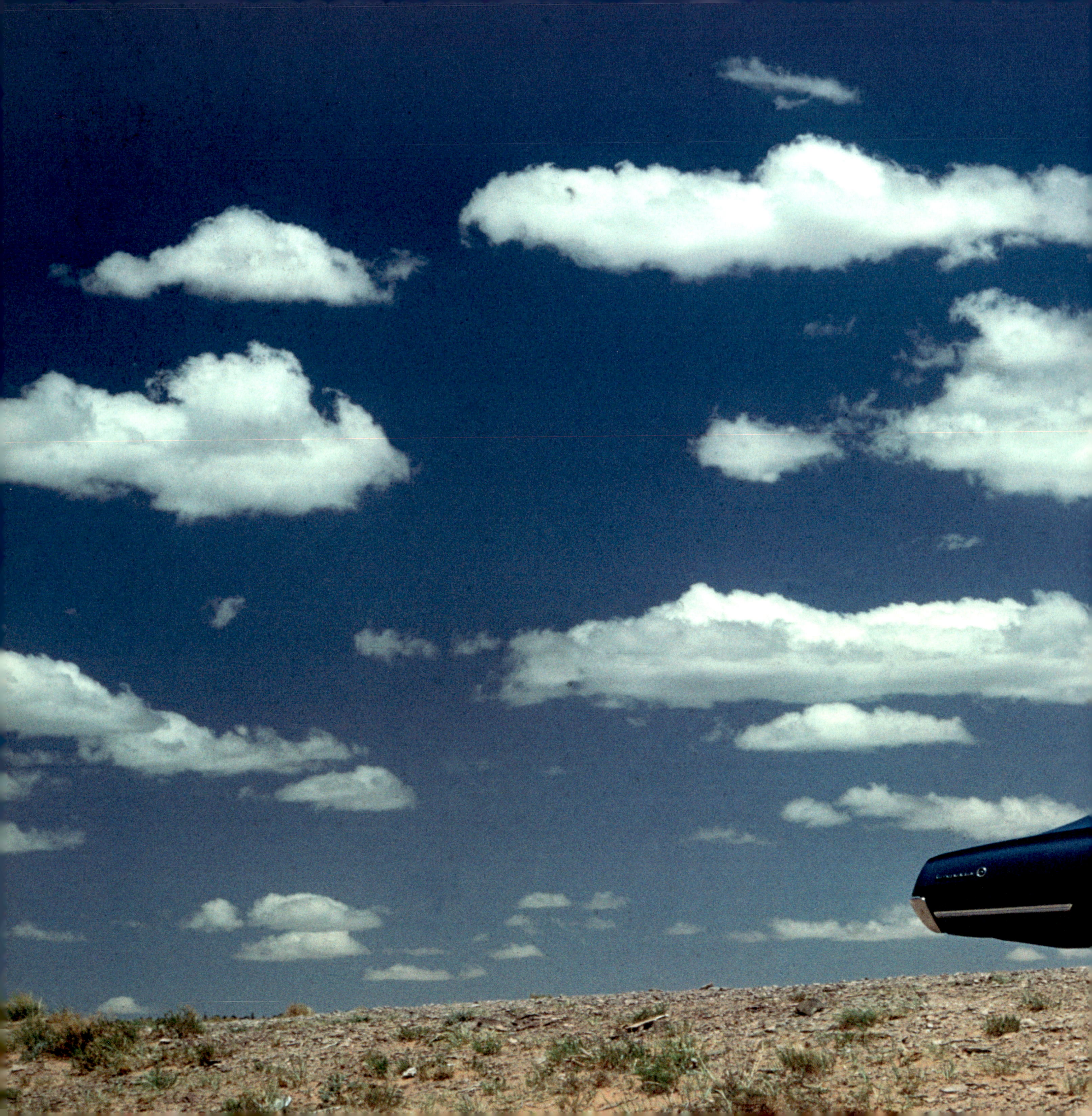

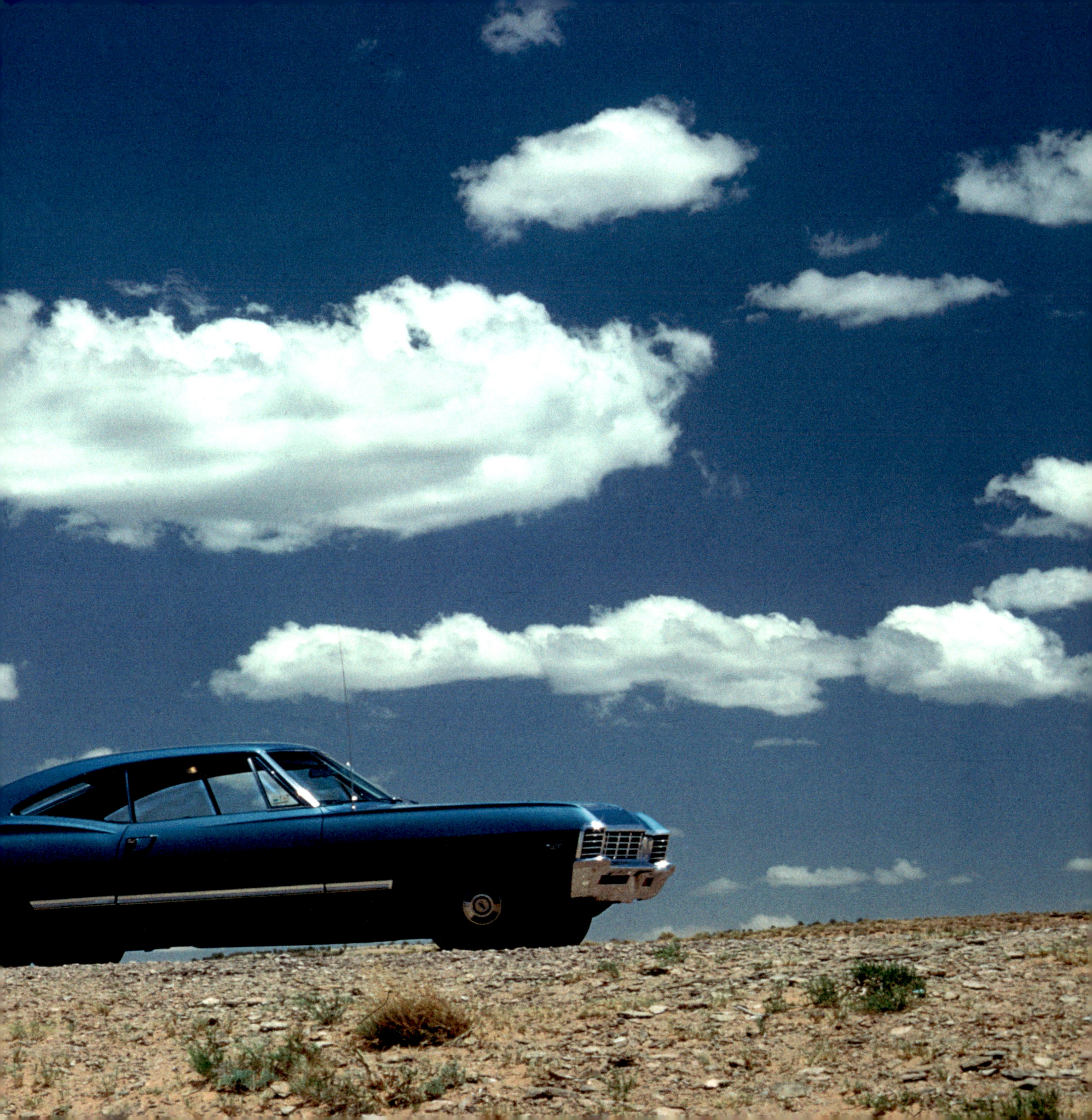

1967 Chevrolet Impala (previous page)
1960 (left) and 1963 Cadillac Eldorado (right)

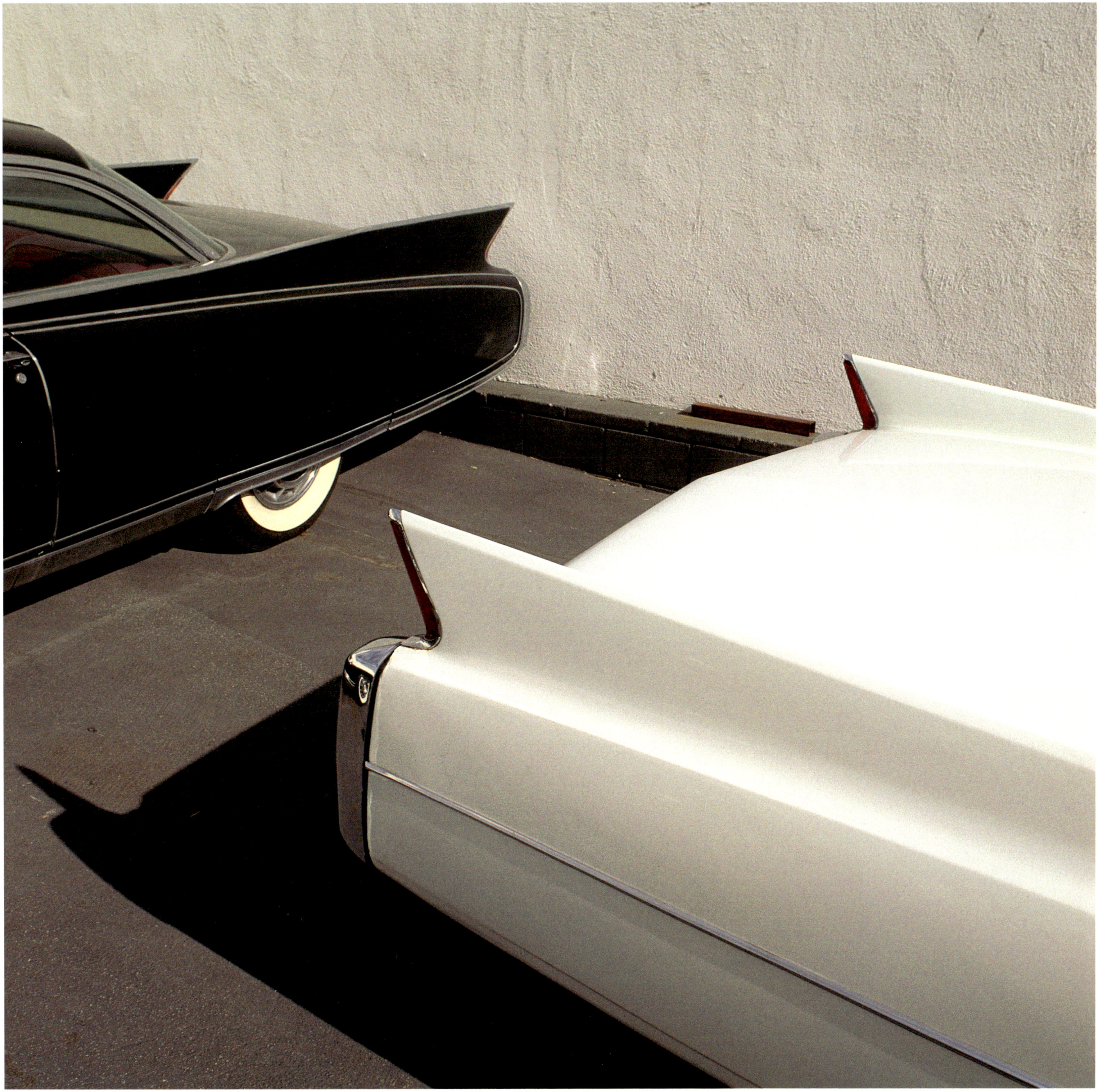

Ford Thunderbird company emblem, 1957

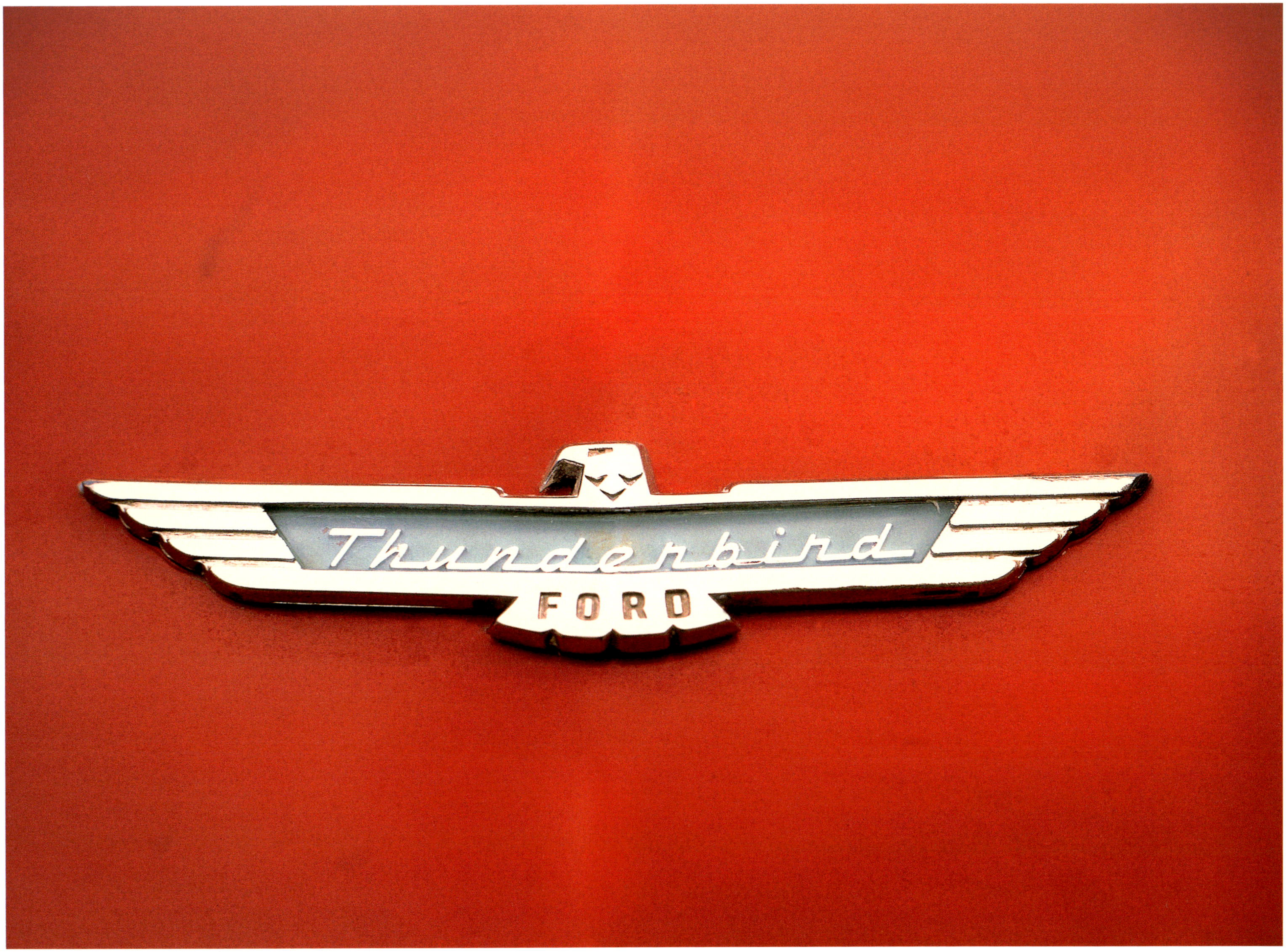
Thunderbird
FORD

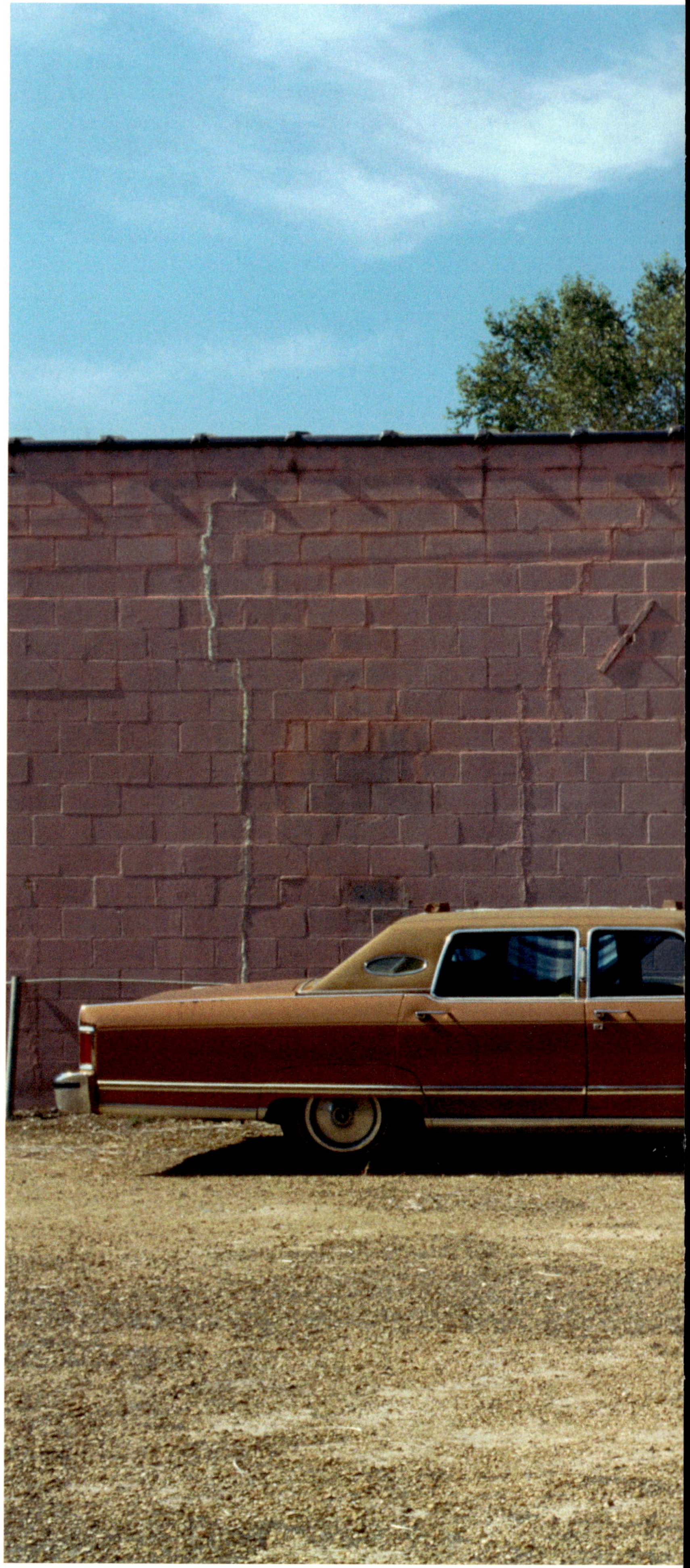

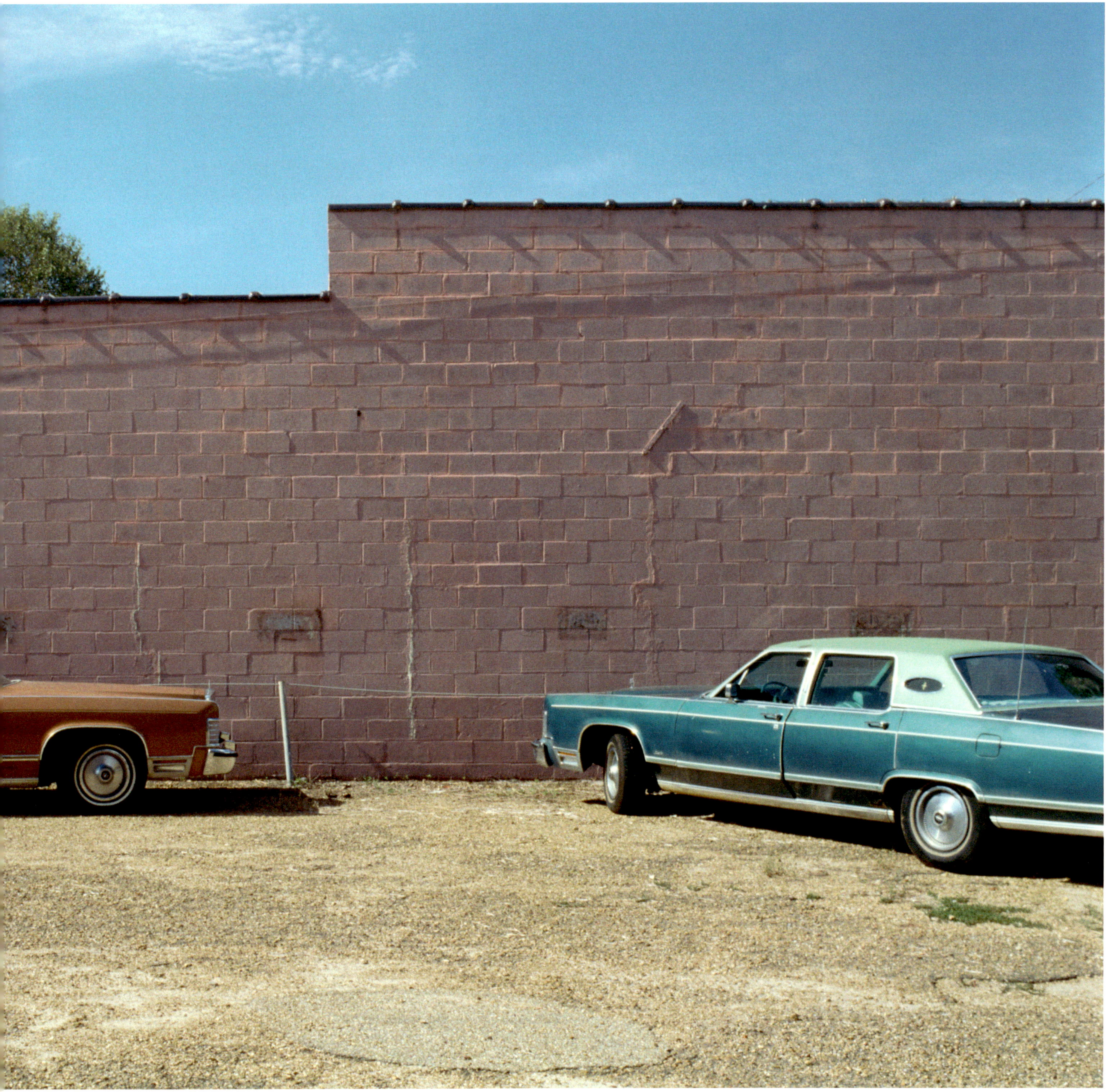

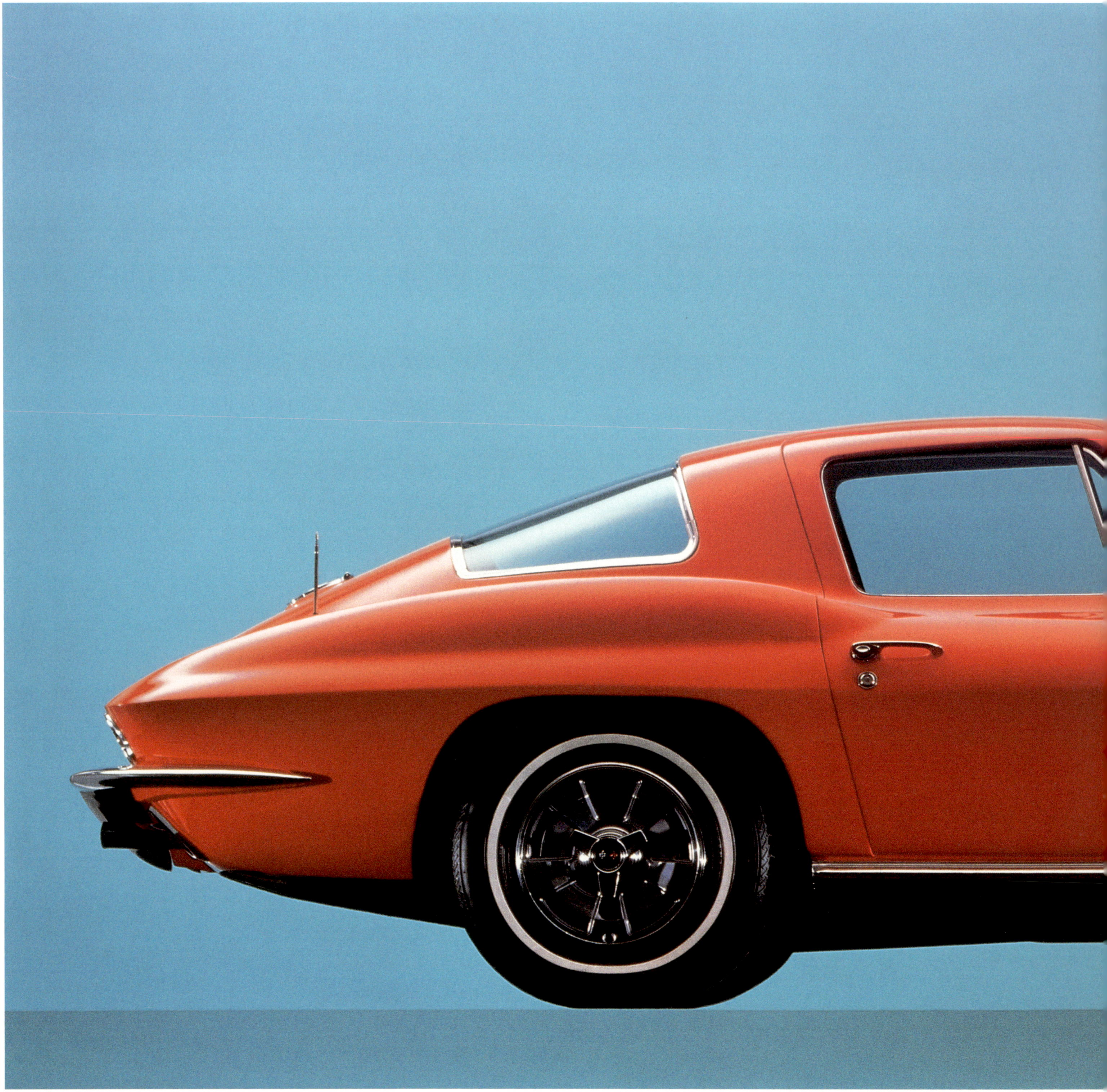

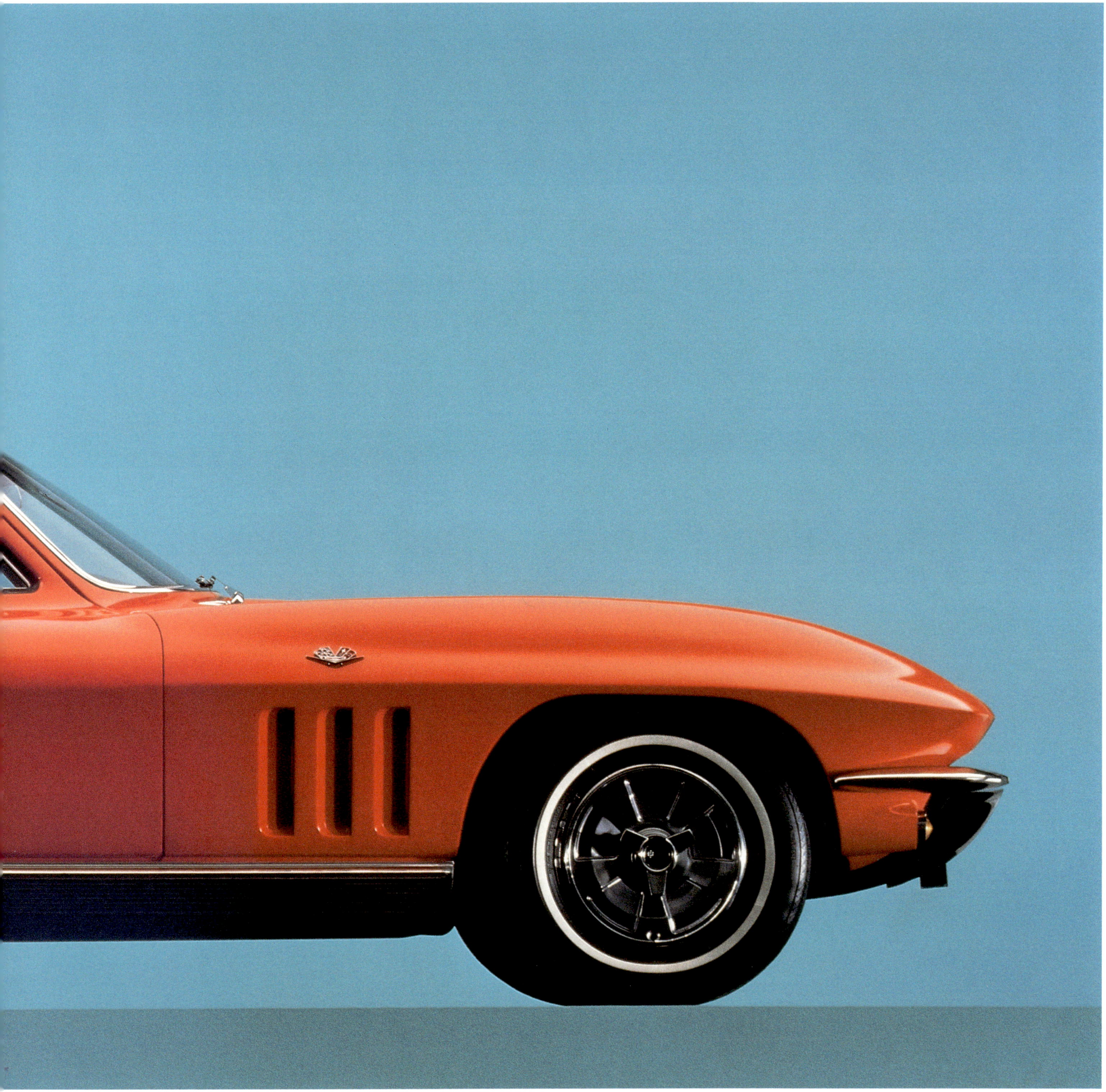

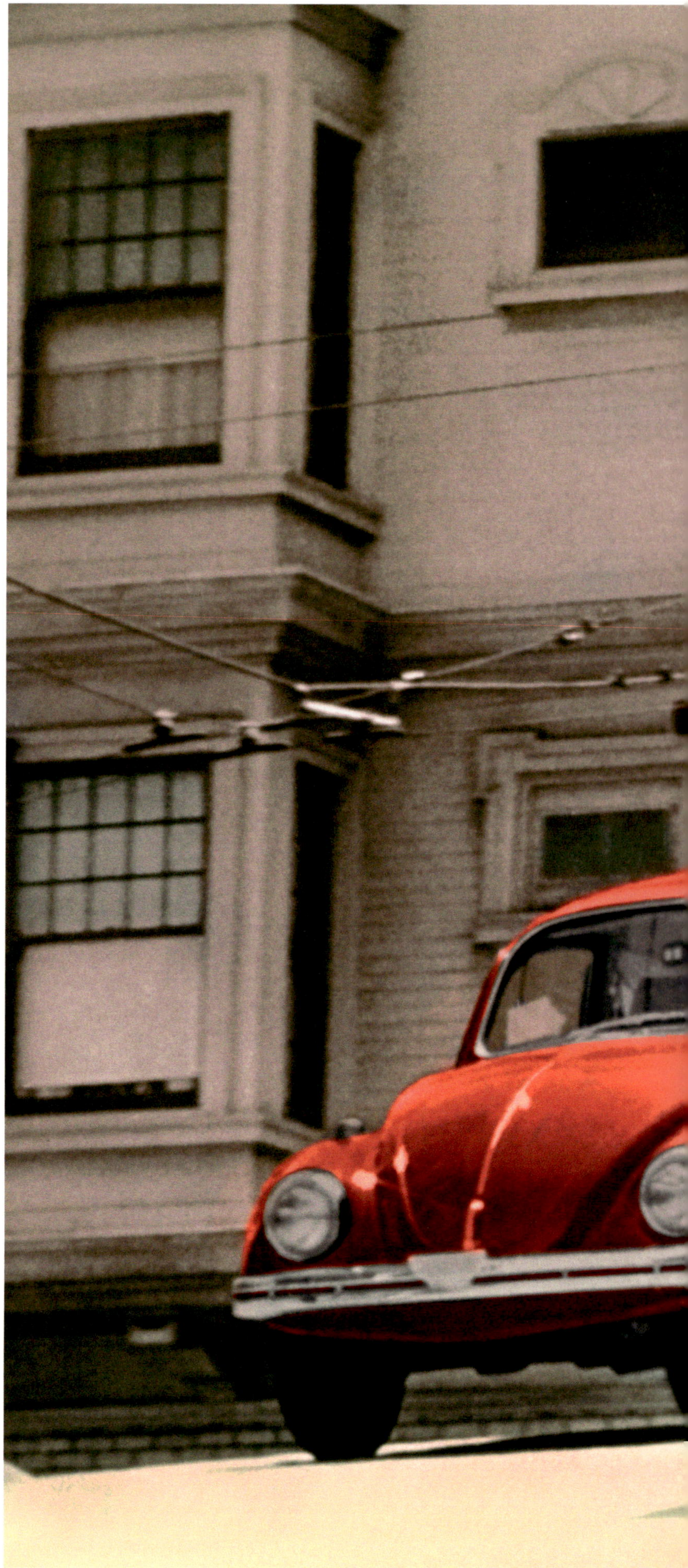

1965 Chevrolet Corvette Stingray (previous page)
A power-packed car: Dodge Charger in a
scene from "Bullitt" (USA 1968, Director: Peter Yates)

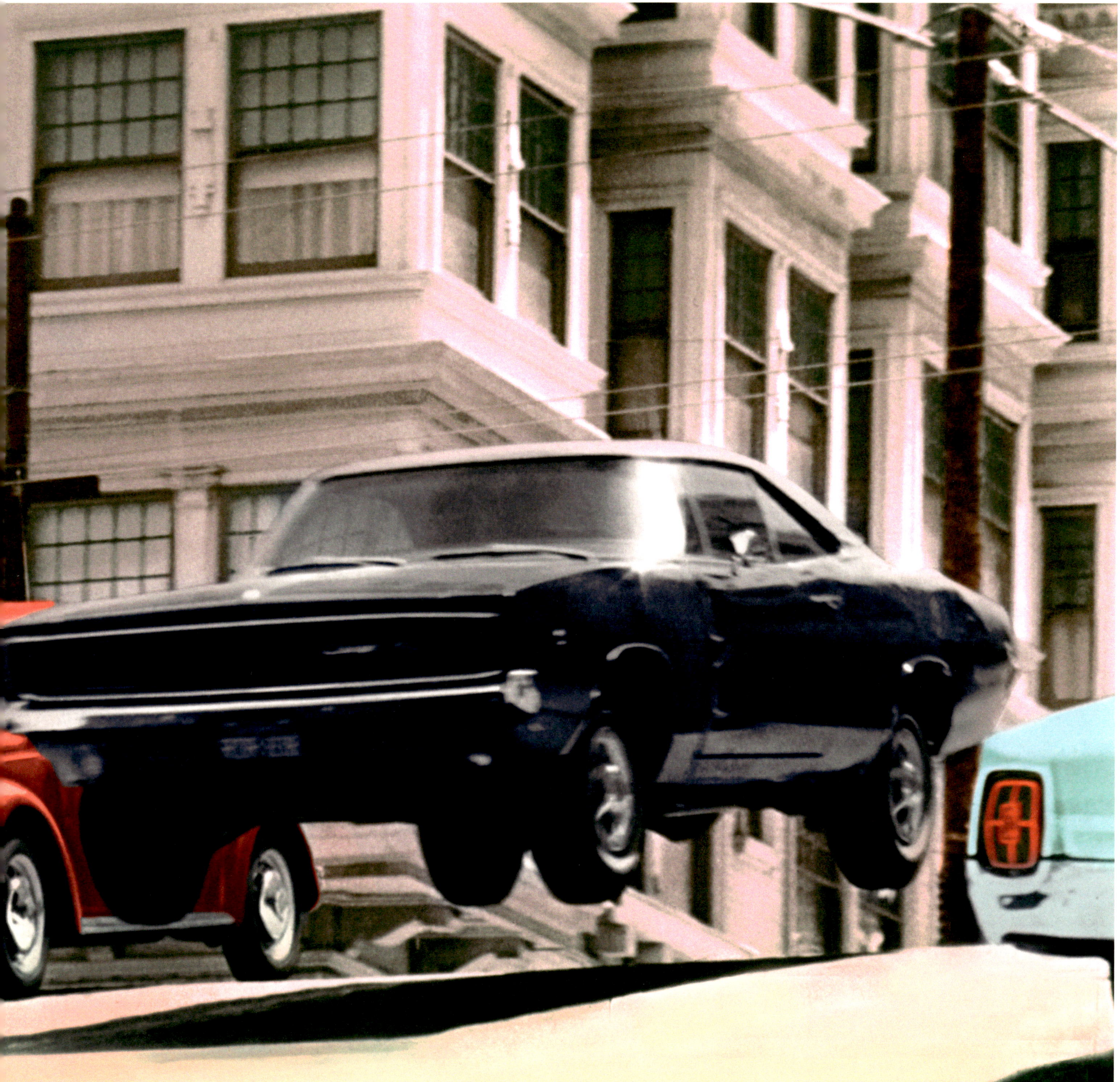

Ford Mustang GTA

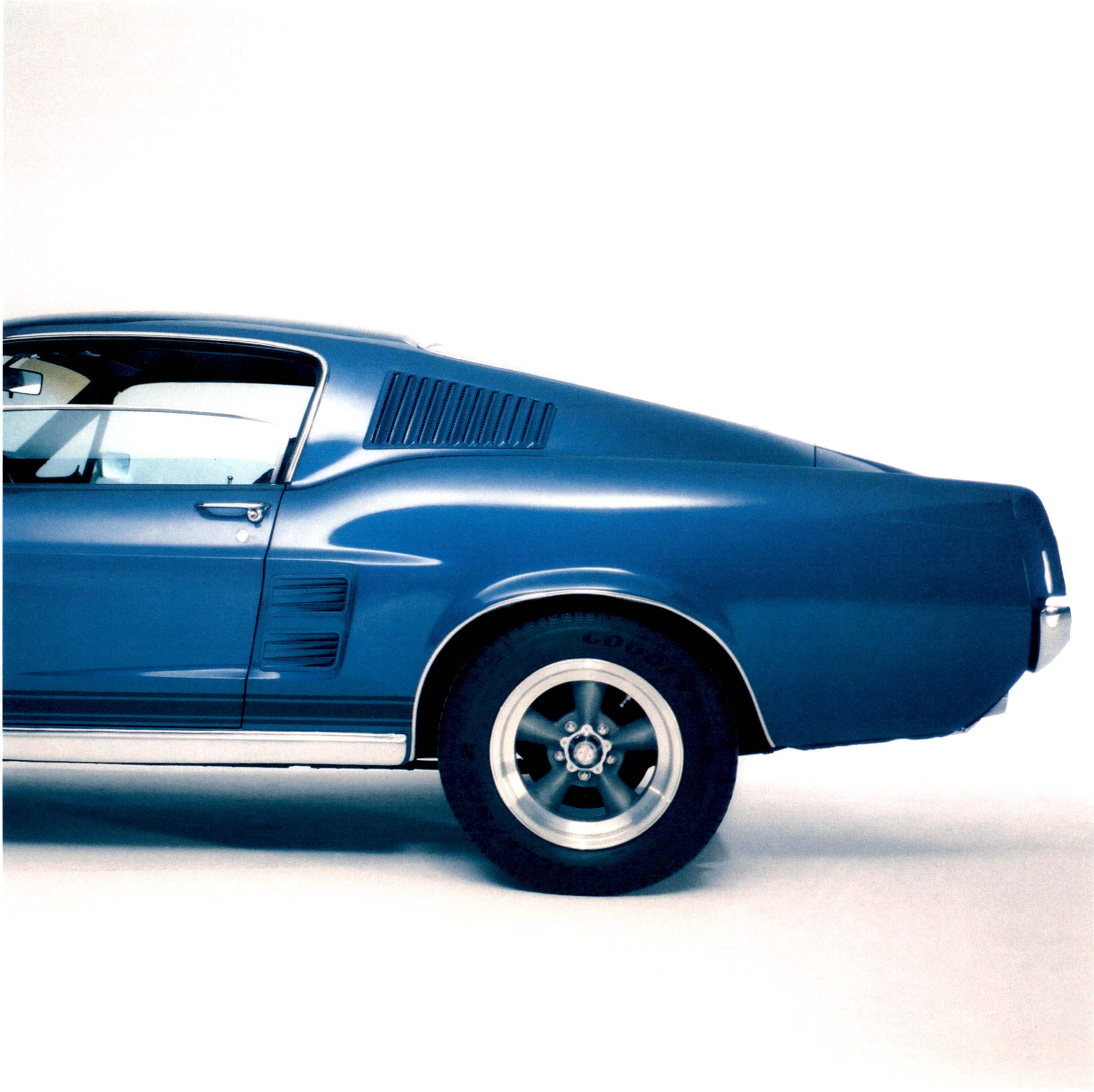

ON THE ROAD, MEN FIND IT EASIER TO SHOW EMOTIONS.

1969 Cadillac Coupé De Ville

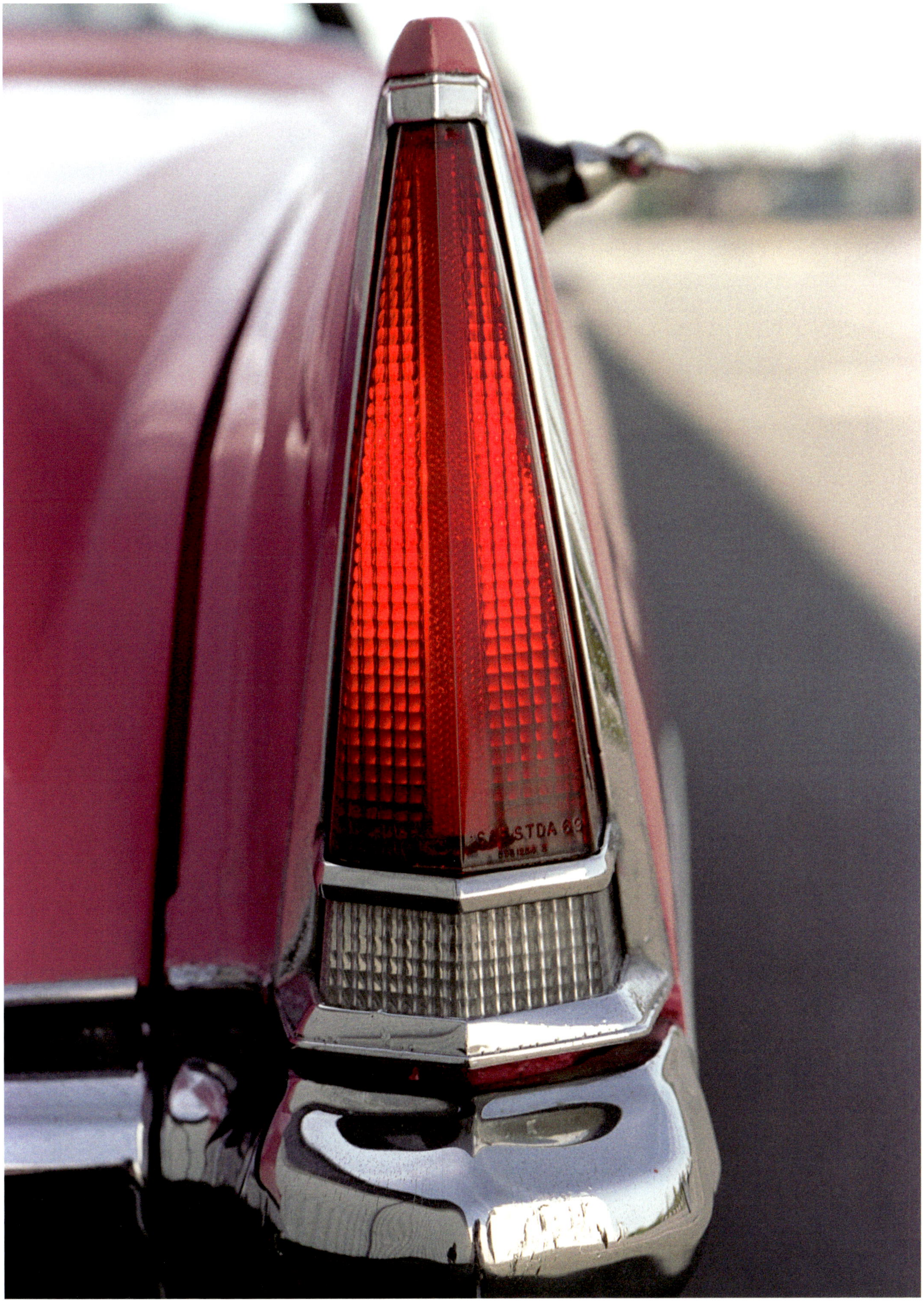

He's a Rebel

CD 01

01 **Crystals** – He's A Rebel 2:17
(Pitney) Super Songs Unlimited / Unichappell Music, Inc. (BMI)

02 **Little Richard** – Tutti-Frutti 2:24
(Labostrie, Lubin, Penniman) EMI Blackwood Music, Inc. (BMI)

03 **The Shirelles** – Will You Still Love Me Tomorrow? (re.) 2:40
(G. Goffin, C. King) Screen Gems-EMI Music, Inc. (BMI)

04 **Gene Chandler** – Duke Of Earl 2:24
(Dixin, Sr. Edwards, Williams) Conrad Music (BMI)

05 **Fabian** – Hound Dog Man 2:12
(D. Pomus, M. Shuman) Music Corporation Of America / Hill & Range Songs (BMI)

06 **Percy Sledge** – (Sittin' On) The Dock Of The Bay 2:34
(Redding, Cropper) Irving Berlin Music Corp. (ASCAP)

07 **Del Shannon** – Runaway 2:31
(Shannon, Cook) Bug Music / Unichappell Music, Inc. (BMI)

08 **Tommy Roe** – Sheila 2:10
(Roe) Low-Twi Music, Inc. (BMI)

09 **Crystals** – Then He Kissed Me 2:35
(Barry, Greenwich, Spector) Mother Bertha Maria, Inc. / ABKCO Music, Inc. / Trio Music Co., Inc.

10 **Betty Everett** – The Shoop Shoop Song (It's In His Kiss) 2:15
(R. Clark) Trio Music Co., Inc. (BMI)

11 **Sandy Nelson** – Let There Be Drums 2:27
(Nelson, Polodor) EMI Unart Catalog, Inc. (BMI)

12 **Jimmy Clanton** – Go, Jimmy, Go 2:06
(Pomus, Shuman) Hill & Range Songs (BMI)

13 **Ray Peterson** – Tell Laura I Love Her 2:53
(Barry, Raleigh) Edward B. Marks Music (BMI) / Music Sales Corp. (ASCAP)

14 **Lloyd Price** – Stagger Lee 2:57
(L. Price, H. Logan) Irving Music, Inc. (BMI)

15 **Little Richard** – Lucille 2:28
(Penniman, Collins) EMI Blackwood Music, Inc. (BMI)

16 **Chiffons** – One Fine Day 2:18
(G. Goffin, C. King) Screen Gems-EMI Music, Inc. (BMI)

17 **Mary Wells** – My Guy 2:48
(Robinson) Jobete Music Co., Inc. (ASCAP)

18 **The Ad Libs** – The Boy From New York City 2:56
(Taylor, Davis) Trio Music Co., Inc. (BMI)

Hey Baby!

CD 02

01 **Lesley Gore** – It's My Party 2:18
(Gluck, Gold, Wiener) World Song Publishing, Inc. (ASCAP)

02 **The Drifters** – Save The Last Dance For Me 2:36
(Pomus, Shuman) Manor Music Co., Ltd

03 **Bruce Channel** – Hey Baby! 2:23
(Channel, Cobb) EMI Unart Catalog, Inc. / Le Bill Music, Inc. (BMI)

04 **Wanda Jackson** – Let's Have A Party 2:20
(Robinson) MPL Communications, Inc. (ASCAP)

05 **Carl Dobkins jr.** – My Heart Is An Open Book 2:16
(Robinson) Casa David Music / Emily Music Publishing Corp. (ASCAP)

06 **Swinging Blue Jeans** – Hippy Hippy Shake 1:48
(Romero) Jonware Music Corp. / Careers-BMG Music Publishing (BMI)

07 **Fabian** – Tiger 2:31
(Jones) Music Corporation of America / Screen Gems-EMI Music, Inc. (BMI)

08 **Foundations** – Build Me Up Buttercup 2:59
(D'Abo, McCaulay) EMI Unart Catalog, Inc. / BMG Songs, Inc. (BMI)

09 **Tremeloes** – Here Comes My Baby 2:55
(Stevens) Angusa Music Co., Ltd / Mainstay Music, Inc. (BMI)

10 **Bobby Rydell** – Wild One 02:21
(D. Appell, K. Mann, B. Lowe) Lowe Music Publishing Corp. (ASCAP)

11 **The Drifters** – Sweets For My Sweet 2:40
(Pomus, Shuman) Trio Music Co., Inc. / Hill & Range Songs (BMI)

12 **Trini Lopez** – La Bamba – Part 1 4:24
(Lopez) Songs Of PolyGram International, Inc. (BMI)

13 **The Coasters** – Poison Ivy 2:44
(Leiber, Stoller) Jerry Leiber Music / Mike Stoller Music (ASCAP)

14 **Chubby Checker** – Let's Twist Again 2:24
(Mann, Appell) Kalmann Music, Inc. (ASCAP)

15 **The Drifters** – There Goes My Baby (re.) 2:12
(Nelson, Patterson, Treadwell) Rightsong Music Co. / Jot Corp. (BMI)

16 **The Cleftones** – Heart And Soul 01:46
(H. Carmichael, F. Loesser) Famous Music Publishing Co. (ASCAP)

17 **Little Richard** – Send Me Some Lovin' (re.) 2:27
(J. Marascalco, L. Price) EMI Blackwood Music, Inc. (BMI)

18 **Diamonds** – Little Darlin' (re.) 2:11
(Williams) AVI Music Publishing Group, Inc. (BMI)

Only You

CD 03

01 **Ben E. King** – Stand By Me (re.) 3:00
(J. King, J. Leiber, M. Stoller) Jerry Leiber Music / Mike Stoller Music (ASCAP) / Hill & Range Songs (BMI)

02 **Brook Benton** – It's Just A Matter Of Time (re.) 2:32
(B. Benton, B. Hendricks, C. Otis) Hudson Bay Music Co. / Trio Music Co., Inc., Eden Music (BMI)

03 **Robert Knight** – Everlasting Love 2:51
(Cason, Gayden) Rising Suns Music, Inc. (BMI)

04 **The Shangri-Las** – Give Him A Great Big Kiss 2:10
(G. Morton) Screen Gems-EMI Music, Inc. / Tender Tunes, Inc. / Trio Music Co., Inc. (BMI)

05 **Tina Turner** – Stand By Your Man (re.) 2:44
(B. Sherrill, T. Wynette) EMI Al Gallico Music Corp. (BMI)

06 **Wayne Fontana** – A Groovy Kind Of Love (re.) 2:02
(Sager, Wine) Screen Gems-EMI Music, Inc. (BMI)

07 **Frankie Avalon** – Just Ask Your Heart 2:29
(P. Damato, D. De Nota, J. Ricci) Rambed Music Publishing (BMI) / Music Corporation Of America

08 **The Association** – Cherish (re.) 3:23
(Kirkman) Beechwood Music Corp. (BMI)

09 **The Platters** – Only You (And You Alone) (re.) 2:38
(B. Ram, A. Rand) Hollis Music, Inc. / Screen Gems-EMI Music, Inc. (BMI)

10 **Jewel Akens** – So This Is Love 2:20
(Howard, Newman) Pattern Music, Inc. / MCA Music Publishing (ASCAP)

11 **Clarence "Frogman" Henry** – (I Don't Know Why) But I Do 2:18
(Guidry, Gayten) ARC Music Corp. (BMI)

12 **Bobby Vee** – More Than I Can Say 2:25
(Curt, Allison) Peermusic (UK) Limited

13 **Shirelles** – Dedicated To The One I Love 2:18
(Bass, Pauling) Duchess-MCA Music Publishing / Fort Knox Music, Inc. / Trio Music

14 **Skeeter Davis** – The End Of The World 2:40
(Dee, Kent) Edward Proffitt Music / Music Sales Corp. (ASCAP)

15 **Betty Everett & Jerry Butler** – Let It Be Me 02:51
(G. Becaud, M. Curtis, Delanoe) MCA Music Publishing Co. (ASCAP) / SDRM

16 **The Platters** – Smoke Gets In Your Eyes 2:36
(Kern, Harbach) PolyGram International Publishing, Inc. (ASCAP)

17 **Percy Sledge** – When A Man Loves A Woman (re.) 2:55
(C. Lewis, A. Wright) Pronto Music, Inc. / Quincy Music, Inc. (BMI)

18 **The Bachelors** – Whispering 02:28
(R. Coburn, V. Rose, J. Schonberger) Public Domain

Surf City

CD 04

01 **Jan & Dean** – Surf City 02:30
(J. Berry, B. Wilson) Screen Gems-EMI Music, Inc. (BMI)

02 **Jimmy Clanton** – Venus In Blue Jeans 2:18
(Greenfield, Sedaka) Screen Gems-EMI Music, Inc. / Careers-BMG Songs (BMI)

03 **The Drifters** – Saturday Night At The Movies 2:36
(Mann, Weil) Screen Gems-EMI Music, Ltd

04 **The Elegants** – Little Star (re.) 2:43
(Picone, Venosa) ABZ Music Corp. (BMI)

05 **The Marcels** – Blue Moon 2:09
(Hart, Rogers) EMI Robbins Catalog, Inc. (ASCAP)

06 **Pat Boone** – Love Letters In The Sand (re.) 2:21
(F. Coots, C. Kenny, N. Kenny) Bourne Co. (ASCAP)

07 **Pat Boone** – Speedy Gonzales 2:38
(Kaye, Hill, Lee) Bienstock Publishing Co. / Larry Spier, Inc. (ASCAP) / Budd Music

08 **Chubby Checker** – Popeye The Hitchhiker 02:31
(Mann, Appell) Kalmann Music, Inc. (ASCAP)

09 **Sam and Dave** – Soul Man 02:38
(I. Hayes, D. Porter) Walden Music, Inc. / Almo Music Corporation (ASCAP)

10 **Frankie Ford** – Sea Cruise 2:45
(Smith) Cotillion Music, Inc. (BMI)

11 **Spanky and Our Gang** – Lazy Day 03:07
(Fischoff, Powers) Screen Gems-EMI Music, Inc. (BMI)

12 **Paul Evans** – Seven Little Girls Sitting In The Back Seat 02:13
(Hillard, Pockruss) Post Music (BMI)

13 **Bobby Sherman** – Bubble Gum And Braces 02:07
(Justin, Sherman) Not Needy Just Greedy Music (BMI)

14 **Four Preps** – Down By The Station 02:35
(Belland, Larson) Beechwood Music Corp. (BMI)

15 **Jimmy Clanton** – Just A Dream 02:26
(Clanton, Matassa) Carbert Music, Inc. (BMI)

16 **Del Shannon** – Little Town Flirt (re.) 2:50
(Cook, Shannon) Bug Music / Mole Hole Music / Unichappell Music, Inc. (BMI)

17 **Hank Ballard** – Let's Go, Let's Go, Let's Go 02:34
(Ballard) Fort Knox Music, Inc. / Trio Music Co, Inc. (BMI)

18 **Danny & The Juniors** – At The Hop 2:40
(Singer, Medora, White) ARC Music Corp. / Six Continents Music (BMI)

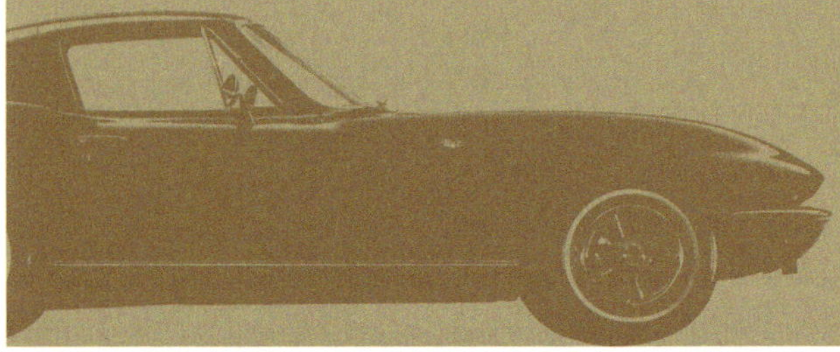

PHOTO CREDITS

PAGE	
Title	IFA
05	Getty Images
06 / 07	Corbis
09	Photonica, Reggie Casagrande
11	Global Picture, Bernhart
13	Cintetext, Sammlung Beyl
15	Getty Images
17	Getty Images
19	Iconica
21	Photonica
22 / 23	DPA, Schneider
25	Zefa
27	Photonica, David Katzenstein
29	Photonica, Charles Daniels
30 / 31	DPA
33	Getty Images
35	Corbis, Elizabeth Chucker
36 / 37	Bilderberg, Frieder Blickle
39	Zefa
41	Getty Images
43	Iconica
44 / 45	Getty Images
46 / 47	IFA
49	Corbis, Richard Cummins
50 / 51	IFA

PAGE	
53	Christian Steiger
55	Christian Steiger
56 / 57	Christian Steiger
59	Christian Steiger
61	Christian Steiger
63	Cintetext, Quade
65	Cintetext, Quade
66 / 67	Getty Images
69	Mauritius
71	Getty Images
72 / 73	Corbis, Gary Thomas Sutto
74 / 75	DPA, GM Media Archiv
77	Corbis, Farrell Grehan
78 / 79	Photonica, Steven Weinberg
81	IFA
82 / 83	Iconica
85	Photonica
86 / 87	Getty Images
89	Corbis, Robert Landau
91	IFA
92 / 93	Photonica, Gerry Johansson (UK)
94 / 95	Mauritius, Kuester
97	Cinetext
99	Mauritius
101	Plainpicture, Meding, D.

TEXT CREDITS

with the exception of
page 24: Lyrics taken from
The Beach Boys – "I Get Around"
(Brian Wilson) Irving Music, Inc. (BMI)

page 28: Lyrics taken from
The Beach Boys – "Drive In"
(Brian Wilson) Irving Music, Inc. (BMI)